He's got the perfect package…

"What is wrong with you?" Samantha asked in complete exasperation. "Can't you just be yourself?"

She hugged herself, feeling like an absolute fool that she'd been taken in by all those lies. He studied her for a moment, and his hands loosened on her shoulders. Good. She just wanted all this weird stuff to—

Suddenly she was flush against his body as one hand pressed the small of her back, the other cupped the back of her head. The kiss was raw and carnal, his mouth claiming hers, his tongue thrusting inside, and heat rushed through her. His stubble scraped her lightly, and her knees went weak. Lord, he was a good kisser. His leg wedged between hers, and she throbbed for him. The kiss went on and on, the delicious friction of his leg between hers had her insides spiraling and tightening. Omigod, she was gonna—

He pulled back, easing his leg from between hers, and looked into her eyes. "That was me."

First Edition: October 2014
Cover design by The Killion Group
Published by: Extra Fancy Books

ISBN-10: 0991266579
ISBN-13: 978-0-9912665-7-9

KISSING SANTA

KYLIE GILMORE

Chapter One

"I am *not* having an arranged marriage," Samantha Dixon told her mother firmly.

This was America.

This was the twenty-first freaking century.

"Don't think of it as an arranged marriage," her mother said, setting a platter in the sink.

They'd just finished Thanksgiving dinner, and the two of them were on kitchen duty. Samantha's older sister, Lucia, got a pass since she was two months pregnant and in the throes of morning sickness. Probably why her mother suddenly felt it important to marry her thirty-year-old daughter off fast. Wilting on the vine and all that.

Her mother raised a finger and smiled. "Think of it as a traditional way to date."

"And marry," Samantha said. "I heard that part loud and clear. Ma, this is ridiculous. This isn't the old country. I don't have a dowry."

Her mother was originally from Mexico, and they didn't even do arranged marriages there anymore. Her mother met her father when he was on spring break in Mexico. It was love at first sight when they met on the beach, as they always liked to say. They married as soon as her father graduated college a month later, and he brought his new bride back with him to

Connecticut. It was *such* a romantic story.

Samantha loved romantic stories. She could *almost* forgive her mother this ridiculous scheme on the theory that it was the thought that counted. Her mother wanted her to have a happy-ever-after like Samantha often dreamed of, inspired by the romance novels she devoured and the countless rom-coms she loved.

Her mother was suspiciously quiet. Samantha looked over. Her mother's lips formed a flat line. She wasn't denying the dowry thing.

"Wait, do I have a dowry?" Samantha asked.

"Of course not, but you do have some savings bonds from when you were born that might sweeten the deal."

Samantha groaned and took her mounting aggravation out on the roasting pan she was washing. "I'm *not* having an arranged marriage."

"Just meet the young man. He's my friend's grandson from a good family."

Samantha scrubbed harder. "No way."

Her mother spoke in her no-nonsense voice. "His mother and I had a nice talk and are in agreement. It's settled."

She dropped the sponge. "*Ma-aa-aa*! I can't believe you! I can meet my own men."

Her mother arched a brow. "Can you?"

Sadly, the evidence didn't back her up. After she was downsized from her graphic designer job in the city last year, she'd moved back home, started working freelance, and effectively killed her love life. She mostly saw her computer, her parents, and her best friend. Her online dating venture ended abruptly when she somehow got on a list for men seeking women with big butts. She didn't even have a big butt, she just had curves. Regular old curves. Hmph.

She'd taken to haunting the aisles of the Home & Tool superstore cruising for men (along with other doomed attempts at romance too numerous to bear thinking about). A typical example—the day she met Diablo, as she liked to think of the tall, dark, and bad boy alpha she'd found in the Sealer and Grout aisle.

He wore low-slung jeans with a faded gray T-shirt that emphasized his broad shoulders. He stood legs apart like he was in command. In charge of the grout section. The badass barbed-wire tattoo circling one huge bicep drew her in.

She stood next to him, holding a basket with a hammer in it. (She always bought a hammer because it was small but seemed important.) She studied the grout display as if she was about to buy one and grout something. She kept sneaking glances at him—black hair a little too long, stubble along his jaw, killer cheekbones, long lashes. He looked just like the cover model of her favorite romance novel *The Alpha Fox*. He looked over. Piercing blue eyes. Swoon!

Then he spoke, a beautiful, dark, rich baritone. "Are you lost?"

"Not at all," Samantha said. "I'm buying grout, but I'm having a little trouble deciding between—" she gave the shelves a quick glance "—the tub or the squirty thing."

He flashed a perfect white smile, and her pulse raced. She smiled back.

He handed her the squirty one. "This one's easier." He gave her a once-over, and Samantha's hopes soared. "You sure dress up for someone buying grout. You got a hot date after this?"

Omigod! Was he asking her out?

She smoothed her hands down her lucky red dress. "No, I don't. I'm single."

He inclined his head. "Lucky you. Live it up while you can. Next thing you know you're spending Friday night buying shit to redo the bathroom for your weekend honey-do project."

"Oh. Yeah, sure." She dropped the grout in her basket.

"Thanks for your help."

She drove home and added the hammer and grout to her ever-growing stash of Home & Tool products in the back of her closet.

Her love life was a joke.

Somehow she'd kept a little piece of her romantic soul after she'd dumped the lying, cheating Tim last year, but with each romantic disaster since then, her hopes plunged further into despair.

"Auntie!" It was her five-year-old niece, Gabriella. The girl in drooping pigtails, a purple dress, and white tights came skidding to a halt in her stockinged feet in front of Samantha. Gabriella panted dramatically and held up a small water sprayer. "I found another monster in the closet upstairs, and I'm all out of monster spray!"

"Don't worry," Samantha said with a wink. "I made a fresh batch."

"Such nonsense," Samantha's mother muttered.

Samantha handed the roasting pan to her mother to dry and took the sprayer from Gabriella. She went to the pantry, undid the nozzle, and pretended to pour some fresh monster spray in. Then she snuck a mini-marshmallow from the bag and handed it to Gabriella along with the sprayer.

Gabriella beamed. Samantha smiled back. Her niece looked so adorable with some of her baby teeth missing. She couldn't wait to have kids of her own. Her niece took off.

Samantha returned to the sink.

"Lucia won't appreciate you rotting her daughter's teeth," her mother said. "That's her third marshmallow since dinner, and she had pie."

"They're mini-marshmallows. Besides, it's a holiday."

"Too much dessert."

Samantha went back to washing dishes. "I'll brush her teeth as soon as I'm done here."

"I want you to give this young man a chance." Her mother shook her finger at her. "You're not getting any younger."

Samantha clenched her teeth. No, she wasn't getting any younger. She'd wasted her college years dating a guy who was super nice and also super boring. When she'd dozed off during sex, she'd finally called it off. Things had been rocky since then. She'd dated a series of nice guys and nearly convinced herself that passion was something only found in the movies because she'd never felt one lick of it, until she met Tim Johnson. His charm and good looks had seduced her into a passionate year-long relationship. That had ended when she'd discovered she was the other woman. Seems his Johnson got around. And how did she find out he was married? His wife answered his cell phone and blasted her and her slutty ways.

The part that hurt the most was…she'd really loved Tim. The rat bastard. Every time she thought of him she got mad all over again. She should've seen the signs—the late-night booty calls, the way he always wanted to go to her place, the way he never said he loved her back. She'd mistaken lust for love. She wouldn't make that mistake again.

Still, some part of her held out hope that there was a guy out there that made her pulse race *and* treated her right. Someone that swept her off her feet and into the sunset. Most importantly, someone that truly cared about her. *Just* her.

Did he even exist?

She exhaled sharply and handed another pot to her mother to dry. Her mother was right. She wasn't getting any younger. Maybe it was time she settled. Passion came at too high a price.

Suddenly she felt depressed. This was what her life had come down to. Giving up on romance. Her mother setting her up. Knowing her mother, the guy was probably a perfect gentleman with impeccable manners and a conservative haircut. In other words, a geek. I mean, what kind of guy needed his mother to set him up?

In a fit of irrational optimism, Samantha decided no, she wouldn't give up on romance, and she would absolutely *not* let her mother take over her love life.

"It's not happening," Samantha said, wishing she had something, anything that could prove she could meet men on her own. Maybe she could make up a fake boyfriend and then break up with him before her parents could meet him.

Her mother didn't take the prize for Queen of Relentless Nagging for nothing. "One dinner is all it will take. He'll be here Saturday night. His mother has assured me of this."

"Ma-aa-aa!" Samantha moaned.

~ ~ ~

"Ma-aa-aa!" Rico del Toro moaned as his mother brandished the Thanksgiving turkey wishbone at him in challenge. "This is silly."

Damn wishbone. It had all started with a fight over it at the kids' table, where he always sat with his nieces and nephews. Their table was way more fun.

"Hey, hey, hey!" he'd hollered at his nephews in battle over the wishbone. "Fighting doesn't make wishes come true. Now who needs a wish the most?"

His four nephews and two nieces all shouted at once. "Me! I do!"

"No, I do!"

"Me!"

"Let's solve this the easy way," Rico said. "Eenie-meenie—"

"I'm the oldest, I get it!" Dylan hollered.

"I do!" Michael hollered back. "I could kick your butt."

Rico raised a brow. Michael made a good point. At eleven, he was a full head taller than his thirteen-year-old cousin. The kids started yelling and talking over each other again. He glanced at his two older sisters, the kids' mothers, who went on ignoring them and talking a mile-a-minute way down the other end at the grown-up table.

His mother, sitting at the head of the table, raised one hand for silence. Slowly, the effect spread all the way down the table as the entire family fell silent. All eyes turned to her. Cristina del Toro's gentle, firm voice carried through the room.

"Rico and I will do the wishbone this year."

Rico's eyes widened. That was strange. He never did the wishbone. Couldn't have cared less about it. "Ma, why me?"

"Bring it here," she said. His mother spoke to him in English only out of politeness for their host. His sister Maria's husband, Steve, only spoke English. Everyone else was bilingual.

He snatched the wishbone from where it was still gripped between Michael's and Dylan's greasy fingers and went to the head of the table. His father sat at his mother's side, content to let her be in charge. Rafe del Toro loved a cold beer and a good joke. His philosophy on marriage was simple: "Happy wife, happy life."

His mother held out her hand for the wishbone, and he gave it to her. "It's time for you to marry."

His jaw dropped in shock. He wasn't even seeing anyone. "Ma, you feeling okay?"

She straightened her shoulders and stood to her full five foot two, holding out the wishbone almost like a challenge. "I'm feeling fine. You, on the other hand, thirty-three and still flitting from one trampy woman to the next—"

"They're not trampy..." He trailed off at the slitty-eyed glare of fire she leveled at him. Hell, he liked easy women. They knew how to have a good time and had zero expectation for more. He'd been in love once, the real deal, even though they'd only been in high school. He'd been crazy about Jamie, had loved her heart and soul, and wanted to marry her as soon as she graduated college. But then once Jamie left for college, things changed. Her phone calls came less frequently. She became too busy on the weekends for him. And then she'd finally dumped him for her new college boyfriend. He hadn't had a serious relationship since.

He left the wishbone hanging out there, unwilling to battle his mother over it. He had a feeling that wishbone was going to bring him some bad juju.

"Do not interrupt your mother," his mother snapped.

"Sorry."

His older sisters, Maria and Elena, giggled. They loved when he got the brunt of their mother's opinionated attention. They always said he had it easy because he was the baby and the only boy. He'd been his parents' surprise baby. His sister Elena was ten years older than him; Maria twelve years. He shot his sisters a dark look that made them giggle even more.

"It's time you settled down," his mother said sharply. "Enough of these wild oats. My friend has the perfect woman for you. I told her you would take Samantha to dinner Saturday night. One dinner is all it will take for you to open your eyes to your future wife. It is *destino*."

He jolted at the wife thing. How had they gone from dinner to marriage? And he wouldn't exactly call it fate to have his mother set him up. He tried reason, though he knew that was a losing battle when his mother had her mind set on something. "I can find my own wife, er, date. I don't need a setup."

The wishbone lowered, and he relaxed.

"No one worth bringing home for your family to meet," his mother huffed. "This girl is Catholic, and her mother brought her up the right way."

He stared at her. "What right way is that?"

"The traditional way."

He held up his palms. "What traditional way? This is America."

Elena and Maria roared with laughter.

"Ricky's getting married," Elena teased.

Even his father was chuckling.

His mother shook the wishbone at him. "If you get the bigger piece, you may do as you wish. If I do, you go on this date with the *right* kind of woman."

Fine. He'd win the stupid wishbone break, and they'd be done with all this traditional woman crap. He couldn't wait to drive back home to Clover Park, Connecticut, and pick up some beautiful woman at Garner's Sports Bar & Grill looking to escape her family. He wanted that fast escape even more now.

He gripped the wishbone. It was really slippery from his nephews fighting over it so long. His mother braced her legs apart like they were about to do battle. Maybe they were. The family went quiet. Even his sisters finally shut their giggling traps.

He pulled and the wishbone snapped. He opened his hand. It was the short end. *Mierda.*

His mother held up the larger end in triumph.

"Finally!" she exclaimed. "Rico will marry and give me more wonderful grandchildren. She is thirty, not too old."

"Finally, Rico!" Maria exclaimed. "Now we can all get on with our lives. You were really dragging your feet there."

His mother shot Maria a quelling look. She immediately quieted.

Rico dropped the short end of the wishbone on the table. *Bad juju.* "I said I'd go on a date, not get married and have kids."

His mother clasped her hands in prayer and looked toward the ceiling. "I pray I don't die before I can meet Rico's children."

He rolled his eyes. His mother was sixty-eight and showed no signs of slowing down. She'd probably meet her great-great-grandchildren.

She gripped his hand. "*Mijo*, listen, this is very important.

Use your best manners. Call her parents Mr. and Mrs. Dixon. None of that funny stuff joking. Be serious. Samantha Dixon does not want a clown."

"Okay, Ma. I'll do that, but I'm not making any promises. One date."

She kissed him on both cheeks, and he flashed to *The Godfather*. It felt about as ominous.

"Now help your sisters clear," she commanded. "Then put away the extra table and chairs."

His father and brothers-in-law chuckled. He shot them a dirty look. "Lotta help you were."

"We're already married with kids," his brother-in-law Steve said. "We did our part."

He blew out a breath and started gathering the kids' plates. His mother always made him help his sisters. Elena and Maria had been like having a second and third mother clucking over him as a kid. He'd liked it sometimes, found it overwhelming at others. But now they didn't coddle him at all. Now they wanted payback—full work from him whenever they snapped their fingers. If he didn't love them so much, he'd revolt.

His mother's gaze fell on the other men. "You men can laugh all the way outside. Go rake all the leaves for Maria. She says they've been sitting there for a month. Kids, follow me!"

Everyone snapped to with a few moans and groans thrown in.

Rico headed for the kitchen, glad he wasn't outside with the men. He spent most days doing the hard labor of landscape maintenance and cleanup as crew chief at his best friend Trav O'Hare's company Elegant Land Designs. He set the dishes in the sink and ran the water. So he'd lost a stupid wishbone break. Big deal. He'd go on one date with what was most likely a very homely, lonely woman who depended on a network of parents to find her dates, and move on. He could survive one dinner.

Chapter Two

Rico rang the bell at the Dixons' house in nearby Eastman right on time on Saturday night. God forbid they report back to his mother that he showed up late. He still couldn't believe he was going out with someone his mother had set him up with sight unseen, but he knew if he didn't go, he'd never hear the end of it.

The door swung open, and he goggled. Standing in front of him was a beautiful, sexy woman. She wore a black dress that hugged her curves, ending mid-thigh with black fuck-me heels. Her hair was dark brown and fell in soft waves to her shoulders. Her skin was smooth like cream. And her mouth—full pouty lips meant for sin. He couldn't believe his luck. This was who his mother picked out for him? He should've let her set him up years ago.

He met her dark brown eyes and saw the same surprise he felt reflected there. He gave her his I'm-very-happy-to-see-you smile that always got a return smile from the ladies. She smiled back, and their gazes locked. Some powerful chemistry sizzled between them, keeping him rooted to the spot. Her gaze dropped to his mouth, and he instantly got hard.

A woman's voice rang out from the house. "Who is it?"

The spell was broken. Samantha stiffened, muttering, "Who do you think it is, Ma?" She stepped onto the porch, shut the door behind her, and pursed her sexy lips. "So you're my date."

The vibe coming off her went from *yeah, baby* to aggravated in seconds. Probably her mother had killed the moment. That was okay. Once he got her to dinner, he'd charm the panties off her.

"Hi, I'm Rico," he said, holding out his hand to shake.

She shook his hand and quickly dropped it. "Samantha."

He nodded. "Nice dress. You look good in black."

She regarded him somberly. "I'm wearing black because I'm in mourning."

"Oh, you are? Who died?"

"My dreams."

He stared at her, confused. "Your—"

"One dinner," she said. "That's it."

Her mother's voice hollered from inside the house, "Bring him in!"

Samantha looked to the sky, and then in the exact same tone of aggravation that he always used when he said the word, she groaned, "Ma-aaa-aaa!"

She looked at him. He gestured inside. She huffed, stepped inside, and slammed the door in his face.

He heard some loud female voices arguing behind the door, and then Samantha stepped outside, holding a black coat and purse, and slammed the door behind her.

He raised a brow. "I take it I'm not gonna meet your mother."

Her eyes flashed at him. "If my mother can sing your praises for three days straight, then she doesn't need to meet you." She marched down the sidewalk and ticked his virtues off on her fingers, only they came out sounding like the worst sins. "You come from a good family. You're Catholic. You have sisters, so you know how to treat a lady. You're respectful to your mother. You have a good job." She pinned him with a sharp gaze. "Did I miss anything?"

He bit back the joking remark that immediately came to mind: *I'm good in the sack.* She was royally pissed at her mother, and he didn't want that falling on him.

"That about covers it," he said.

They arrived at his truck, and he opened the passenger-side door for her. "You have a beautiful name."

She heaved a sigh. "My mother has the crazy idea that she and your mother have agreed on an arranged marriage between us."

She got in the truck, and his eyes trailed down to her curvy ass. Her words suddenly sank in. "Wait, say what?"

She smirked. "News to you, huh? The groom is always the last to know."

He shut the door and walked slowly to the driver's seat. Every alarm bell was ringing in his head over that arranged marriage deal. He considered opening her door and setting her free. They didn't have to go along with what their mothers said. He thought his mother with her married-and-kids talk was just doing her usual wishful thinking. Their mothers actually thought they'd arranged a marriage?

He slid into the driver's seat and glanced at her. Her jaw was clenched tight as she stared out the front window. A woman with that much fury could be channeled into passion. Her dress rode up higher now that she was sitting down, exposing even more shapely leg. Nope, he wouldn't mind that passion directed at him at all.

He pulled out of the driveway. "Look, as long as we agree our mothers are meddling busybodies that we can ignore, it's okay for us to go out."

"You think it's that easy?"

"Yeah."

"You don't know my mother."

He paused. He knew his mother, and if hers was anything

like his, that meant a lot of follow-up. If the date went well, his mother would want to know when the wedding was. If the date went badly, his mother would want to know what he did wrong. Damned if you do…

"Well, we gotta eat," he said. "You like Italian?"

"Let's just get some fast food and call it a night."

"No can do. I've got reservations." He headed over to Lombardi's, a nice restaurant that he'd been to a few times when he wanted to impress a date. He hadn't wanted word getting back to his mother that he was cheap. Though usually all he had to do was buy a girl a drink.

"Okay, fine," she said. "Here's the deal. I'm telling my mother that you're in love with someone else. You tell your mother the same. Then we'll pretend we have someone on the side that we'll break up with just before anyone can meet them. Okay?"

"I'm not pretending I have someone on the side," he said. "She'll be all over that."

"Just do it! There's no better way." She frowned. "I've been over all the angles," she added grimly.

He stopped at a red light. "Can't we just say we didn't get along?"

Her eyes lit up. "Perfect! That way it's nobody's fault. We'll just say we didn't click."

"You have beautiful brown eyes."

"Thank you, Rico, but you don't have to keep giving me compliments. This is a onetime deal to get our mothers off our backs. One dinner, back home again, and done."

Rico held his tongue. He wasn't going to argue for more than one dinner. One date was usually all it took for a very successful evening. He had a lot more compliments stored up that worked very well for him, but he'd wait until she was more agreeable after some wine. He just needed to loosen her up a bit.

~ ~ ~

Samantha forced herself not to look at Rico's handsome profile as he drove to the restaurant. It was bad enough his musky cologne wrapped itself around her in the confines of the truck, making her want to reach over and taste…No. Absolutely not. This guy had player written all over him. And while her body had reacted to meeting him with a resounding *Hello, let's fuck like rabbits!* (a natural biological instinct any woman would've had upon meeting him), her brain knew better. She had him pegged the minute he showed up on her doorstep, all confidence and swagger and good looks. He knew he was good-looking, too, with that caramel skin, deep brown eyes, and stubble along his jaw. Not to mention a voice that could've been on the radio it was so smooth and melodic. Oh, and the fact that he hadn't even zipped his leather jacket so she'd notice right away the way he filled out the dress shirt.

Nice touch, play-uh.

Rico parked, opened her truck door, and walked her into the restaurant. She relaxed as she stepped inside. The place was festive and cheerful, decked out for the holidays with greenery and twinkling white lights along the ceiling, archway, and windows.

The hostess, a gorgeous brunette with cleavage on prominent display in her barely buttoned shirt, practically purred at Rico.

"Long time no see." The woman walked around the hostess stand to kiss him on the cheek while letting her breasts rub against his arm.

Rico slung an arm around the hussy. "Miss me, darling?"

"Like an itch that needs a scratch…" She leaned in and whispered something in his ear, then bit his earlobe.

Rico chuckled. "You're so bad. I've got reservations for two. This is Samantha."

The brunette glanced at Samantha dismissively. "Right this way."

After she showed them to their table, the woman had the nerve to lean down to Rico, showing off a clear view down her shirt, and whisper, "Call me."

Rico winked, and the woman strutted away, hips swaying.

Samantha stifled a groan.

"Nice place, huh?" Rico asked, all innocent and clueless.

"Yeah, nice," she muttered.

She took a deep breath. She just had to get through one dinner. Be polite. Pretend it didn't matter that her date was a complete man-slut. That only mattered if they were a couple. Which they never would be. She focused on the warm and cozy atmosphere of the restaurant. A pianist on a baby grand in the corner played gentle Christmas music. Each round table held a glowing candle.

Rico opened up the menu. "Should we order some wine?"

"No, thank you," she said.

The last thing she needed was to let her defenses down and fall prey to his womanizing ways. She'd get through this dinner stone-cold sober if it killed her.

He gave her a slow, sexy smile that she steeled herself against even as her insides turned to mush. "That really is a pretty dress."

"Thanks," she said dryly. She had to let him know she was immune to all his false flattery. "I like your shirt too," she added. "Nice buttons."

He raised a brow and rolled up the sleeves, revealing muscular forearms. *Oh no, he didn't.* Her mouth went dry. His moves were so obvious they really should have zero effect on her. Thankfully, the waiter showed up to tell them about the specials, giving her a reason to tear her gaze away from Rico's muscles.

The waiter left, and Rico picked up right where he left off.

"You look beautiful by candlelight."

She pursed her lips and stared him down. "Everyone looks beautiful by candlelight. You can barely see me."

"Something wrong?"

She was about to say, *Yes, something's wrong! My mother set me up with a blind date who turns out to be the one kind of man I never want to be with again! Been there, done that, got the devastating heartbreak.* But his attention wasn't on her. He waved to someone across the restaurant. She turned to see the hostess blowing him a kiss while she seated another couple.

"Would you like to get better acquainted with our hostess?" she asked sweetly.

He turned and gave her that slow, sexy smile again. This time she felt nothing but aggravation. Okay, a little tummy flutter, but whatever.

"I want to get better acquainted with you," he said. "How did I get so lucky to be set up with a beauty like you?"

She was too mature to stick her finger down her throat in a gagging motion, but she wanted to. Badly.

"The usual way," she said. "I had no choice in the matter."

He barked out a laugh. Flustered, she stared at her menu, debated just walking out, and thought better of it with the fallout she was sure she'd get from her mother upon her early arrival home.

The waiter came to take their orders. She chose a salad so it would be a quick meal.

Things went downhill from there. He spent the entire evening giving her all these super fake compliments about her glossy hair, her deeply thoughtful eyes, her devastating smile, her dainty wrists, even her graceful fingers. Seriously, she knew she wasn't model beautiful. Obviously these lines worked on some women, but to her they just sounded like the worst kind of phony talk.

They lapsed into awkward silence. He must've sensed his

phony lines weren't going to get him anywhere. Finally she couldn't take the silence anymore.

"I need to use the ladies' room," she said, excusing herself.

She stood in the ladies' room, wondering how she got to such a sucky place in her life. Single, living at home, letting her mother direct her love life. After she felt she'd waited long enough for him to finish his meal, she touched up her lipstick and returned to their table.

"You want dessert?" he asked.

"I want to go home."

He signaled for the check and turned to her. "Let me ask you this, if you had met me any other way, would you be interested?"

She narrowed her eyes suspiciously. "Interested in what?"

He gestured up and down his body.

Argh! Samantha threw down her napkin, grabbed her coat and purse, and stood. "Take me home. Now."

He pulled out his wallet, left some bills on the table, and they headed out the door.

Samantha jammed her arms into the sleeves of her coat. She couldn't spend one more minute sitting across from that big phony. As if that wasn't enough, she had to endure uncomfortable silence followed by him propositioning her. He probably wanted to make out in his truck in front of her parents' house.

They walked in silence to his truck.

"We're not kissing good night," she informed him.

He stopped walking. "You really don't like me, do you?"

He actually looked hurt, and she was swamped with sympathy. "I'm sorry. I'm sure you're a very nice person in some ways. I mean, you do love your mother or you wouldn't be here with me, right? I'm just not liking this whole deal. Let's leave it as friends and go on with our lives."

They continued on in silence. He opened her door for her.

That was nice. He *was* rather gallant.

"I don't have women friends," he said before shutting her door.

She waited for him to get in. "Why not?"

He put the truck into gear. "What's the point?"

"What do you mean what's the point?"

"Never mind," he said quickly. They headed back toward her parents' house.

"No, I really want to know. Why is there no point in having a woman friend?"

He kept his mouth shut.

I know your type all too well.

"You use women for sex and that's it," she said.

"I don't use women. We use each other." He looked over at her lecherously. "And everyone comes out happy, I assure you."

"You're a sexist pig."

"How is that sexist? I said we use each other. Believe me, the women I sleep with are *very* satisfied. Haven't heard any complaints."

"Because you're already outta there. You've probably broken hearts without a backward glance." Her throat got tight. "Just know that when two people sleep together, the woman's heart is involved *big time.*"

He glanced at her curiously. "Is your heart broken?"

She'd said too much. "I'm just speaking in general." She crossed her arms, hugging herself. "On behalf of my gender."

"I really do like that dress," he said with a leer at her now pushed-up cleavage.

She dropped her arms. "Shut up."

He shook his head. "I have no idea why our mothers thought we'd make a good couple."

A flash of hurt went through her, and she instantly tamped it down. He was right. They wouldn't make a good couple. But she wanted him to think she was a catch, even if she thought he was a sexist pig.

She lifted her chin. "I have no idea either. They're insane."

He laughed, a deep, rolling laugh that warmed her and had her laughing too.

"You got that right," he said.

When they got to her parents' house, Rico turned off the truck, got out, and opened her door again. At least his mother had taught him some manners.

He walked her to the front door and extended his hand to shake. "I guess this is good-bye forever."

A stab of regret went through her. Would things have gone differently if they hadn't been forced together? No, he was a player, and she'd already had her share of those.

She shook Rico's hand, and just like the first time, a hot tingle ran up her arm. She quickly dropped his hand. "Good-bye forever, Rico. Thank you for the salad."

He grinned, flashing a perfect white toothy smile. The man could do commercials for whitening strips. "Thank you for the beautiful view."

Before she could come up with some snappy reply, he turned and strutted down the front walk. She clenched her teeth. Major player. She was lucky she'd seen him for exactly what he was.

Chapter Three

One week later, Rico headed back to his apartment after work, looking forward to his usual Friday night hanging out at Garner's Sports Bar & Grill. He almost always went home with a new phone number in his pocket or a woman on his arm. He was glad all that Samantha business was finished. He'd told his mother he'd been on his best behavior, but they just didn't get along. His mother had been surprisingly sympathetic to him. Maybe Samantha's mother had told her how difficult Samantha had been. All of his usual compliments and charm had seemed to irritate her. Hell, no one could've gotten through that major attitude.

He stopped short at his front door. A note was taped to it. Strange. The note asked him to stop by his downstairs neighbor's apartment "for a quick visit." The older man, Harold, had always been friendly and helpful, but they'd never hung out.

When he arrived at his neighbor's door, a middle-aged woman answered. "My dad is sick and can't do his gig as Santa at the pancake breakfast tomorrow. He's so sorry to miss it. He loves playing Santa every year. He asked if you could take over."

Rico put both hands up and slowly backed away. "I'm no Santa."

He was a young, fit, non-jolly man with a rep for being good with the ladies. Definitely not Santa material.

She thrust the red Santa suit and white curly wig and beard into his hands. He pushed it back.

"It's from nine to twelve at the high school," she said. "Just go to the cafeteria. You'll get breakfast out of it."

"I can buy breakfast."

"Please, my dad doesn't have many friends. You were on his emergency contact list."

"I was?"

She thrust the red suit into his hands again. Then she handed him a glasses case. "Yes. And this is an emergency."

He pushed everything back. No way was he dressing up like a jolly old elf.

She gave him a pointed look. "Ficus."

Rico groaned. He knew that would bite him in the ass one day. But, come on, Santa? His parents had given him a ficus tree to celebrate his new job at Trav's landscape company ten years ago. He'd kept it alive all these years, liking the reminder of his family and how proud they'd been of him. He'd grown sort of attached to that tree and asked Harold to water it whenever Rico was away. Harold had done so for the past ten years, refusing payment or anything in return. Now Harold was calling in that favor. Argh.

"Give it to me," Rico said, holding out his arms. "Then tell him we're even."

A guy like him playing Santa was much worse than ten years of looking in on a ficus tree.

She grinned, dropped the outfit in his arms, and shut the door. He looked down at the red velvet suit with the huge white beard. *Ay Dios mio.* And ho-ho-ho.

So it was that Rico found himself putting on the big red suit early Saturday morning. He told no one and prayed no one recognized him. It would just be a bunch of kids, he reassured himself. He stuffed a pillow down the front to look more like ol' St. Nick. He went to the bathroom mirror and put on the beard, wig, and Santa hat and burst out laughing. There was no way he could pass for the pasty, white-skinned Harold. He put on the round spectacles. Nope. Still looked like Santa Stud. Couldn't be helped. Ah, well. It was just a few hours. He didn't want to disappoint all the kids.

He got in his truck and drove to Clover Park High. He was sweating already. He should've waited to change when he got there. He always ran hot, even in the winter. The wig was itching like crazy over his short-cropped hair, but he was afraid if he showed up half dressed, he'd ruin the magic for the little ones, so he suffered through it.

When he walked into the cafeteria, he was greeted by the joyous sound of The Boss, Bruce Springsteen, belting out "Santa Claus is Coming to Town" over the loudspeakers. He bobbed his head in time to the music. If you had to play Santa, no one better to have sing about it. Rico was from Jersey, and in Jersey The Boss was king. None of the kids had shown up yet. He checked the big clock on the wall. Fifteen minutes until they officially opened.

He breathed in the scent of brewing coffee and pancakes and took a moment to appreciate how Christmasy it looked in here for the kids. His nieces and nephews would love this. There was a large wooden throne with dark green velvet cushions at the far end of the cafeteria, sitting on a frayed red rug. That must be for Santa. Near the throne was a Christmas tree twinkling with multicolored lights, silver garland, and red ball ornaments. An angel perched on top of the tree. Taped to the wall nearby was a painted fireplace. All the long cafeteria tables alternated red and green tablecloths, with a bowl in the center filled with round peppermints with candy canes hanging off the edges. He grabbed a mint. Might as well have fresh breath for the kiddies.

He spotted Shane O'Hare, Trav's younger brother, and his fiancée, Rachel Miller, getting breakfast started in the back. He debated braving the ridicule for a cup of what he knew would be awesome coffee. The pair owned Something's Brewing Café in town and brewed the best coffee he'd ever had. A few volunteers he didn't know were running around setting out plates, utensils, cups, and assorted condiments.

"Oh, look, Santa's here! Hi, Santa!" Rachel waved.

He walked over. "What's up?"

"Rico?" Shane asked. Then he cracked up.

Rachel peered at him. "You're Santa?" Then she cracked up too.

"Very funny," Rico said. "I'm helping out my neighbor Harold. He was too sick to do it. Can I get some of that coffee?"

"Wouldn't you prefer hot cocoa?" Shane asked.

"And cookies?" Rachel asked.

They dissolved into laughter.

"Forget it," Rico huffed. "Geez, try to do the right thing. I'll be over here on my throne." He headed over to the large velvet throne, ignoring their peals of laughter.

Barry Furnukle from The Dancing Cow, a frozen yogurt shop in town, showed up in a green elf costume complete with pointy shoes with bells on them and a pointy hat. Rico felt a little better about the Santa duds.

"Merry Christmas, Santa," Barry said. He peered closer. "Rico?"

Rico sighed. "Yeah, it's me."

His brows scrunched together. "I never expected you—"

"Yeah, yeah, yeah."

Barry stood straight as a soldier. "I'll be your helper and photographer."

"Great," Rico said. "Nice costume."

Barry preened and did a little jig that had the bells on his pointy shoes jingling. "Thank you. So I thought I'd let each kid tell you what they want; then I'll take the picture and bring them over here." He gestured to the side where he had set a large basket. "I'll give them a coloring book, crayons, and a coupon to The Dancing Cow."

"Awesome." Rico shoved a hand under the wig and scratched. "How many kids show up for this thing anyway?"

"This is my first rodeo, so I don't know. We'll be ready for anything, right, Santa?"

"Right. Do we get a break? You know, to feed the reindeer or something?"

"Let's do a fifteen-minute break halfway through."

He wiped some sweat off his brow and readjusted the Santa hat. "Yeah, okay. Oh, I see some kids. Get ready."

He settled himself on the throne and tried to look jolly. Should he smile? Nah, he'd better save it for the cameras, or he'd be smiling for three hours straight. He waited. The kids came running in all at once, followed by parents pushing strollers with little ones dressed in red dresses and little suits for their holiday pictures.

The first kid ran over to him and climbed up on his lap. It was a boy, probably about four.

"Ho-ho-ho, what's your name?"

"Tenny."

"Okay, Tenny, what would you like for Christmas?"

"Not Tenny! Tenny!"

"Okay, um, what would—"

"It's Tenny! Tenny!" The boy was working up a good shade of red.

Rico looked to the boy's parents. His mother rushed forward. "It's Kenny. He has trouble with his Ks."

"Okay, Kenny, what would you like for Christmas?" He smiled encouragingly.

"I want wego staw waws pace tip commandaw, wego staw

waws, *blah, blah, blah*…" The kid went on and on. Rico had no idea what he was saying. Santa lost his smile, and his eyes started to droop.

"How about a picture?" Barry asked, giving Rico a little shake.

Rico nodded. Barry raced over to the camera he'd set up on a tripod. He held up a squeaky cow toy above the camera. "Moo-ry Christmas!"

Rico smiled into the camera. The boy scampered off with Barry elf. Rico's eyes widened at the line that had formed in the meantime. Was three hours enough to get through all these kids?

The next family approached. He got one preschooler on each knee, and the mother placed the baby in the crook of his arm. The baby burst into tears. Rico sighed. This job sucked.

Many, many crying babies and kids pulling his fake beard later, he went for his fifteen-minute break. He had to tell Barry to stop saying Moo-ry Christmas. It was wearing on his last nerve. And was it just him or was "Jingle Bell Rock" on repeat on that playlist? He feared he'd never get it out of his head. He wanted The Boss back.

"How's Mrs. Claus?" Ryan O'Hare, Trav's older brother, asked when Rico passed him on the way to the locker room.

Rico scratched his beard with his middle finger and kept going. He heard Ryan chuckle in the distance.

He ripped off the hat and wig in the locker room and scratched his head like crazy. Harold owed him big time for this. Ficus tree or not. He couldn't believe Harold volunteered to sit in an itchy wig and sweltering suit every year. If he had to hear one more request for a pony, he'd puke. No one was getting a freaking pony! He stripped down to his boxers and fanned himself with the Santa hat. His fifteen minutes passed way too quick, and he reluctantly put the suit back on and returned to his throne. First thing, a toddler with a full diaper that could've wiped out a herd of ponies was placed on his lap. Could this gig get any worse?

Trav O'Hare, his best friend from way back (way, way back, they met in kindergarten in New Jersey, making him more like a brother), stepped up with his one-year-old son, Bryce. Rico tensed. He was sure Bryce would recognize him, and Trav would never let him live this down. Trav's wife, Daisy, stopped Trav and adjusted a little Santa hat on Bryce's head. Trav placed Bryce on his lap. His friend did a double take when he recognized Rico under all that velvet and white curls.

Trav burst out laughing. "Wait, wait," he gasped out. He pulled out his cell and snapped a picture.

"Shhh," Rico said.

Bryce stared at Rico and patted his face. The boy definitely recognized him. Rico smiled.

Bryce bounced up and down. "Ree-Ree!" he squealed. At least he couldn't talk that well yet.

"Tell your daddy to shut it," Rico whispered.

Trav couldn't stop laughing. Tears came out of his eyes he was laughing so hard. Daisy gave Rico an apologetic look and pulled Trav away so Barry could take the picture.

As if that wasn't bad enough, next up was Maggie O'Hare, Trav's grandmother. She wore a red velvet dress with a black sash and knee-high black boots. He hoped she wasn't auditioning for the role of Mrs. Claus. Why she wanted to sit on Santa's lap at her age was beyond him. But he forgave her for her kooky ways because she was light enough not to hurt his legs, and, much more importantly, she'd taken him in like family when he moved to Clover Park for the job at Trav's company.

"Oh, Santa, I've been really nice this year," Maggie said. "I made a lot of people happy and set up a lot of love matches, but what I really want is more great-grandbabies. Can you please use your Christmas magic to tell my grandsons to get busy?"

He choked back a laugh.

She turned. "Is that you, Rico?"

"Shhh. Yeah. Harold was sick."

She winked. "I won't give your secret away. Now I'll tell you a little secret. You're next on my love-match list. I already took care of Ryan, Trav, and Shane."

Her three grandsons. This was one time he didn't want to be family. He already had his mother arranging marriages for him. And what a disaster that had turned out to be. Samantha Dixon, despite her stunning beauty, was definitely *not* the one for him.

"Ho-ho-ho!" he exclaimed jovially. How could he politely get her off his lap? A line of kids were waiting to see him. "No need for that, ma'am. I'm married to Mrs. Claus."

"Mmm-hmm." She patted his arm. "I'd also like some new fuzzy handcuffs. Jorge lost the key to the last pair."

Rico cleared his throat. "Is that all, ma'am? We've got lots of other children waiting their turn."

She smiled sweetly. "Thank you, Santa. I can't wait to meet the future Mrs. Claus."

She turned, smiled for the camera, and left with a coloring book.

He let out a breath of relief. Some bigger, heavier kids showed up, and his legs ached from all the weight on them. They asked the tough questions—Are you really Santa? Where's your reindeer? How long did it take you to get to Clover Park from the North Pole?

He checked the clock. Half an hour to go and still a long line of kids. When he got out of here, he was gonna rip off all his clothes and jump into a cold shower. He felt like he'd lost ten pounds between the suit and the kids. It was like a freaking steam bath in this velvet straitjacket.

The last thirty minutes dragged on and on and on until finally there was only one kid left. His jaw dropped. It was a little girl in a red dress with her hair in pigtails, but that wasn't what had him gaping. Next to the girl was Samantha from the date from hell. Was Samantha a single mother? His mother had left out *that* important detail. Geez. Samantha didn't even glance his way, her focus was solely on the little girl, so Rico took his time admiring the way Samantha's pink fuzzy sweater clung to her rack and her black jeans and black high-heeled boots showed off her shapely legs. She wasn't too tall; he always checked that first when he met a woman. He was five nine and a half, and she was still a good inch shorter than him in heels. Damn, he really would've liked to feel those legs wrapped around him just once. If only the woman hadn't been so freaking surly.

The girl ran over and climbed in his lap. She beamed at him, revealing pearly white baby teeth with a few gaps.

He found himself smiling back despite his hellish morning. "Ho-ho-ho. And what's your name?"

"Gabriella."

"And what do you want for Christmas, Gabriella?"

She cupped her hand over his ear and whispered, "A puppy."

He nodded. At least it wasn't a pony. Maybe she'd get one.

"Ho-ho-ho, we'll see what we can do in our workshop." He faced the camera. "Smile."

They smiled for the picture. Gabriella got her coloring book and ran to Samantha. "Your turn, Auntie, tell Santa your secret Christmas wish."

Auntie. That was better than mother. Despite the long morning and his aching legs, he found he wanted to stay a little longer. He wanted Samantha on his lap.

Samantha bent down to Gabriella's level and smiled. "That's just for kids, silly."

Gabriella looked up at her with wide, innocent eyes. "How else will your wishes come true?"

Samantha straightened, looking thoughtful.

He crooked his finger at her.

~ ~ ~

Samantha looked at her niece's pleading eyes and blew out a breath. Oh, what the heck. Harold was a good sport. Look how he was inviting her over. She'd met him several times already at the Santa breakfast. She always went with her sister and Gabriella to the pancake breakfast, only this year her sister's morning sickness kept her away. Her sister would take Gabriella to meet Santa at the mall later. Harold probably wouldn't mind if she made a Christmas wish. Lord knows, she could use one.

"Okay, sweetie," Samantha said. "Wait for me at that table." She pointed to where she wanted her. "Go ahead and start coloring."

Gabriella skipped away. Samantha walked over and plopped down on Santa's lap. She took comfort from the fact that she couldn't quite see Harold's face under the hat, wig, and huge beard. She focused on a pretty snowflake decoration across the room. It was almost like going to confession with Father Jensen, very private, just the two of them. The cafeteria was nearly empty now, except for a few volunteers cleaning up. Even the elf had taken off.

"Oh, Santa, I know it's silly, but I always dreamed of a sweet romance like you read about in books and see in the movies. It just doesn't seem to be happening for me. And believe me, I've tried to move things along." She sighed. "It just seems like everyone's already married or gay or divorced with a lot of baggage. I just want to meet my Prince Charming, you know?"

At Santa's continued silence and good listening, Samantha confided all the heartache she'd endured over the last two years due to her failed romance attempts. First she told him the worst—the Tim Johnson affair—just to get it off her chest and explain what started her on her quest for romance. Then she moved on to the day her hair and makeup were ruined in the August heat while she waited for a mysterious Mr. Hunk to arrive on the scene to change her flat tire (and yes, she confessed, she'd let the air out on purpose) and how a toothless old lady had arrived instead to inform her she had a flat. She'd had to change the tire herself, ruining her white skirt and new heels. She told him of the British hottie who moved in next door to her parents' house that looked a little like Hugh Grant—she'd loved him in *Bridget Jones's Diary*—and just when she was thinking they might really be moving from borrowing sugar (she had a huge stash now) to actually hanging out, his boyfriend showed up.

She sighed and continued on with the advice she took from her friend to look for someone at a wedding and how that had turned out to be a second cousin she'd never met. "Luckily my mother told me before things moved off the dance floor," she whispered.

Santa merely grunted, so she went on. "Online dating was horrible. All those men cared about was my…well, let's just say it wasn't working out." She blew out a breath. "I have a huge hammer collection from all my trips cruising the aisles of Home & Tool for an eligible bachelor. I could never use them all." She shook her head. "Besides, those guys are all married." She straightened, suddenly indignant. "And the worst, my mother tried to set up an arranged marriage with this total player who was too handsome for his own good. He was all—" she waved her hands in the air "—look at me! Don't you want some of this sugar? And I was all, get away from me, you phony! The *lines* that came out of this guy's mouth! If my mother had known what he was really like…" She exhaled sharply. "Don't get me started on my mother."

Finally, she wound down.

"This was all my niece's idea," she said with a rueful laugh. "Since I'm here…my Christmas wish is to meet a handsome, smart, charming man that will just make my head spin with the happiness of true love." She warmed to her topic. "Make him be someone who brings me flowers and candy just because, writes poems for me, serenades me, and likes to hold hands while we go shopping, ice skating, or maybe even walking along the beach." She let out a dreamy sigh. "I guess that's too much for one Christmas wish."

Santa's voice went low and husky. "I'll see what I can do."

Her eyes flew to his, and she took a good look at the guy she'd just spilled her guts to. He smiled, and her hand went to her throat. This man didn't have wrinkles, pasty white skin, and blue eyes. This wasn't Harold! This was someone much younger with caramel skin and brown eyes behind those spectacles.

Santa was coming on to her!

She leaped off his lap and jabbed a finger at him. "You're Santa. You can't pick up women. You're married to Mrs. Claus."

Dear Lord, what had she just told this complete stranger? Her cheeks burned.

The Santa-Harold imposter stood and raised his palms. "I'm off duty. You want to get a cup of coffee?"

She whirled and hurried over to her niece. "Come on, Gabriella, we're going."

"Bye, Santa!" Gabriella called. "Merry Christmas!"

"Ho-ho-ho, Merry Christmas, Gabriella! I'll make sure the elves know about your Christmas wish and yours too, Samantha!"

She froze. Omigod. He knew her name. She'd never said

her name. And that voice. Her mind quickly put the pieces together, that beautiful caramel skin, the brown eyes. It was her horrible blind date—Rico.

She took Gabriella's hand and speedwalked to the parking lot. Samantha had never been so embarrassed in her life. She buckled her niece in, muttering to herself about the nerve of some guys.

They drove home, and Samantha prayed she never, ever ran into that Harold imposter again.

Chapter Four

Rico went straight to the locker room and peeled off the Santa suit he'd taken a sauna in all morning. The experience had gone from okay to flat-out horny with the curvy, beautiful Samantha dropping into his lap and sharing her dreams with him. Women didn't usually confide their dreams to him. Probably because he never spent much time talking to the ladies. He preferred physical action. But Samantha's confession intrigued him.

She was a romantic at heart. So was he. He'd written twenty ballads all about love on his guitar. That might be something she'd be interested in if he could convince her to see him again. He grabbed the Santa outfit and headed for his truck.

A short drive later, he stopped at Harold's apartment to drop off the Santa duds. His daughter answered the door.

"You should take this to the dry cleaner," Rico said. "I sweated off ten pounds in there."

She nodded. "How did it go?"

"Not so bad," he said, thinking of Samantha. "Actually, it turned out pretty good."

"We really appreciate you stepping in. Thank you so much. My dad will be very happy to hear it."

"You're welcome."

"Merry Christmas, Rico," she said.

He smiled, actually feeling in the Christmas spirit even though it was still three weeks away. "Merry Christmas."

He headed to his apartment. After a shower and a late lunch, he thought again of Samantha. He wanted to see her again. He wanted to make her Christmas wish come true. If Santa didn't, who would? He thought for a minute. Should he call and ask her out or just show up?

He grabbed his keys. Definitely show up. Prince Charming would ride up on his white horse and wow her in person. He got into his white Dodge Ram, at least the color was right. And it was a ram. Close enough. He stopped at a florist and bought a dozen roses.

As he drove, he came up with a plan of action. This was his second chance, and he wasn't gonna blow it. He had the flowers. Unfortunately, his only idea for a poem was: You're beautiful, and I want you. That was probably too spot-on. He wasn't so good with poetry. What else had she told him she wished for? Holding hands while doing stuff. He could do that. He'd take her ice skating, and they'd hold hands, then he'd take her to dinner and finish the night at his place with a serenade on his guitar. She did mention a serenade. Lucky for her, he was a singer-songwriter.

A short while later, he pulled into the Dixons' driveway and took a deep breath, hoping Samantha would be nicer after their little talk. He wouldn't compliment her. He'd just do all that stuff she told him about. Now that he wasn't wearing the big red suit, he could properly charm her. That suit had set him back a bit. What girl wanted a guy in a velvet suit with a huge belly full of jelly?

Her house was decorated now with white icicle lights along the roofline, red bows on the lampposts, and a wreath on the door. He should get a tree or something for his place. He usually spent Christmas either with Trav's family or, every other year, with his family at his sister Elena's house. His family was all spread out. His parents had moved back to Puerto Rico, Maria was in Virginia, and Elena in Florida. They alternated getting together every other year, so his sisters could also spend Christmas with their husband's families. This year he'd be in Connecticut.

He rang the bell, holding the flowers behind his back. Samantha answered. He let out a breath of relief. He really didn't want to explain what he was doing here to her parents. They'd be on the phone with his mother in a heartbeat, and he didn't want to get into all that. He was here despite his mother, not because of her.

Her eyes widened, and she looked around the yard behind him like he had his reindeer stashed somewhere. "What are you doing here?"

"I want to make your romantic dreams come true," he said in all sincerity.

Her cheeks turned a pretty shade of pink. She covered her face with her hands and groaned. "I never should've told you all that stuff."

"I'm glad you did. No one's ever told me their dreams before. I want to make yours come true."

She dropped her hands and narrowed her eyes. "Why?"

"I find you intriguing."

"Intriguing," she echoed.

"Yes." He produced the roses with a flourish. "For you."

"Oh!" She reached for them and buried her face in them, closing her eyes and breathing them in.

He got hard just watching her. This Prince Charming stuff was really working on her. And to think if he hadn't played Santa, he never would've known. He sent a silent thank you to Harold.

"They're wonderful!" She met his eyes and smiled softly. His heart did an uncomfortable flip-flop. "Let me put them in a vase, and I'll be right back."

"I'll be here."

~ ~ ~

Samantha went inside, the roses clutched in her hand, feeling an odd combination of excited and wary. She loved the flowers, she'd only been given roses a few times, but she was still wary of Rico. He was a total player. Never mind the fact she was still mortified over what she'd confessed to him earlier.

She sighed. She should tell him thank you but she wasn't interested. It just wasn't worth falling for another player. The last thing she needed was to be one of a long line of women in Rico's life.

She pulled a vase out of the top kitchen cabinet and heard her mother gasp behind her.

"What is this?" her mother exclaimed, rushing forward to where Samantha had left the roses on the counter. She scooped them up and breathed them in just like Samantha had.

"Rico brought me roses. He's out front."

"Where are your manners, Sam? Leaving a man out in the cold."

Her mother set the roses on the counter and turned to let him in, but Samantha grabbed her arm. "Ma, please. Just leave this to me."

She planted her hands on her hips. "What are you going to do?"

Samantha filled the vase with water, unsure how to answer.

"He must really like you. Of course you should go out with him again." Her mother grabbed the roses. "Shoo. I'll take care of this. Go to him."

Samantha didn't move. "I think I'm going to tell him to leave. I don't want to encourage him."

"Of course you do. You must encourage him, or he won't

return." She arranged the flowers in the vase with a big smile. "I told you it's all arranged. He's doing his part, and now it's time for you to do your part."

Samantha gritted her teeth. Again with the arranged marriage stuff?

"Ma, I have no idea what he's doing here again." *Other than my mortifying confession that I wish my very own Prince Charming would bring me roses.* "But I'm pretty sure he's not here because his mother told him to do his part."

"Fine. Don't see him." She waved her hand toward the door. "Leave him out in the cold. Just don't come crying to me when you're single and alone at forty."

She winced. That hit her where it hurt. Forty was a good ten years away, but still. Ouch.

Then her mother nailed her point home. "You and me, we will enjoy our old age together watching *Dancing with the Stars.*"

"Okay, fine, I'll give him another chance!" Samantha exclaimed.

Her mother nodded. "You will thank me for this."

Samantha turned, rolled her eyes when she knew her mother couldn't see it, and went to the door.

~ ~ ~

Rico rocked back and forth on his heels on the front porch and reminded himself not to compliment Samantha, even though she was so, so beautiful. Of course he thought all the women he slept with were beautiful. He loved women, period. Nothing was more beautiful than the female body with all its soft curves.

She popped back on the porch and smiled. It dazzled him, that smile. She was even more beautiful when she smiled. His mouth went dry, and his heart did another weird flip-flop. Maybe he was dehydrated from all that sweating. His heart had never felt so weird before.

"What do you want to do?" she asked.

He cleared his throat. "I thought we'd go ice skating, then dinner, then back to my place for some music. I play the guitar."

"Sounds wonderful," she said in a dreamy voice.

He kinda knew how she felt. Now that she was smiling at him, his brain was a little fuzzy and his heart kept doing these weird palpitations. He hoped he wasn't getting a heart attack for Christmas.

He extended his arm and gallantly walked her to his white ram.

~ ~ ~

All of Samantha's embarrassment over confessing her romantic dreams to Rico vanished that afternoon when he made them come true. She should've confessed what she really wanted to the guys in her past. He was positively princely, and she was loving it. When they got on the ice at the outdoor rink in town, he took her hand. And she felt it, even through their gloved hands, a zing that shot up her arm and made her warm all over despite the cold winter air. They skated past other couples and families while cheerful Christmas music played in the background. Just outside of the rink stood a large pine tree wrapped in multicolored lights. It was the perfect holiday scene. One time she took a turn too fast and fell, and Rico scooped her up and made sure she was steady. And when he returned their rented skates, he came back holding a candy cane he'd bought for her. Swoon!

It was just like being in her very own rom-com, minus the embarrassing comedy stuff. Now he was taking her to her favorite Chinese restaurant. They settled at a table covered in a white tablecloth and snacked on fried noodles while they waited for their food to arrive.

"So how does Prince Charming act romantic at dinner?" he asked with a smile. "I'm new to all this."

That smile was amazing. She forgave him for being too good-looking because she was enjoying his transformation into Prince Charming so much.

She smiled back. "We hold hands and have quiet, intimate conversation."

He reached across the table and held her hand. His hand was rough and calloused and warm. Her insides melted thinking of those rough, calloused hands on her body.

"What kind of work do you do?" she asked.

"Your mother didn't hand you my résumé?"

She laughed. "I tuned her out."

He grinned. "I'm crew chief at a landscape design company. I make sure the crew gets their work done, and I help with the work too. Mowing, excavation, planting, sometimes we'll do some hardscaping. You know, sidewalks, patios, retaining walls. Stuff like that."

She turned his palm and rubbed her thumb across it. "I could tell you work with your hands."

He raised a brow. "You like that."

She smiled. "Maybe."

Their food arrived, and she released his hand. As they ate, she told him about her work as a graphic designer and found him to be extremely attentive. She told him about her hobby painting with acrylics and how she wished she could make a living at it. She marveled over the changes in him. The first time they'd gone out, she hadn't found him to be all that attentive. Now she felt like everything she said was gold. Was this all a dream? She couldn't believe the change in him just because she'd spilled her guts when he was Santa. She felt flushed and giddy as they talked easily about their families and their crazy mothers.

They finished their dinner, and Rico paid, leaving a generous tip. He was even a good tipper. She'd worked as a waitress through college and knew how wonderful that really was. He took her hand and walked her to his truck, where he did that whole gallant gentleman thing again, opening her door and shutting it behind her.

He turned the ignition, blasting the heat, and turned to her. "My place?"

Her heart started pounding. It was a little early to sleep with him. On the other hand, it was technically a second date. And she wanted him. "Um…"

He tucked a lock of hair behind her ear. "I want to serenade you."

She smiled dreamily. "I would love that."

He smiled. "Good."

He pulled out of the parking lot. She breathed deep of his musky scent and looked her fill while his attention was on the road. She wanted to run her hand over the stubble on his jaw, feel it rough against her when they kissed. And they *would* kiss good night this time.

They drove back to his place while Samantha marveled over this new side of him—sweet, attentive, romantic. Maybe this was why her mother thought they would be a good match. She immediately forgave her mother for her matchmaking. She felt giddy. She couldn't wait to hear her first ever serenade.

Chapter Five

Rico was really digging how well all this Prince Charming stuff was working out for him. He wished someone had clued him in earlier. Here he was with the beautiful Samantha, about to get lucky on their second date. Not that he hadn't done that before. Hell, most of his first dates ended up in his bed, but he suspected Samantha normally took a few more dates than that. She couldn't resist his newly romantic ways.

He poured them both a glass of wine—he had a cabinet full of white wine for just such an occasion—and joined her on the sofa.

"Thank you," she said.

"You're welcome." He didn't touch her. That was part of his seduction routine. He waited until they were loosened up from the wine before making his move—a kiss that started at the neck and ended against the wall. He took a sip of wine and got his acoustic guitar from its case where it sat in the corner of the living room.

He returned to her and tuned it. Women loved his guitar. It was why he'd learned to play in high school. No need to chase the ladies once he pulled this bad boy out. They flocked to him. He strummed a few notes and looked over at her. "I write all my own songs."

Her eyes widened. "You do? Wow! I can't wait to hear

them." She tucked her leg under her and settled back to listen.

Already loosening up. Excellent. He wouldn't have to play his full repertoire. Maybe three songs and he'd make his move.

He launched into the first ballad, "*Mi Corazon Roto.*" In English, "My Broken Heart." He sang in Spanish because he felt in Spanish. Also, it impressed the hell out of women. They found the foreign language sexy. He let his voice rise and fall tenderly over the words that built into the achingly beautiful chorus. He glanced half-hooded eyes over to see how much his serenade was rocking Samantha's world.

She blinked rapidly like she was fighting back tears. Was she that moved by the music? Cool. He kept going.

He'd nearly finished the song when she held up her hand. "*Callate la boca.*"

He stopped playing. *Que?* Did she just tell him to shut his mouth?

"What did you just say?" he asked.

She set her wine down and pointed at him. "You stop right there, you-you player!"

"What's wrong?"

"*Mi corazon roto,*" she spat. "Oh, boo-hoo-hoo. I don't want to hear one more word about your beautiful blond sweetheart that got away."

His jaw dropped. "You speak Spanish?"

That set her off. She let him have it in Spanish. Didn't he know anything about her? Didn't he know her mother was from Mexico through the Latina grapevine that got them together in the first place? How dare he bring her here and try to seduce her with songs about another woman!

He set his guitar aside and crossed to her, ready to apologize, but she was still coming at him, jabbing him in the chest. Somehow the Spanish made it worse. Like she was under his skin speaking his language. She didn't look Mexican. Sure, she had dark brown hair and dark brown eyes, but her skin was so light. She must take after her father.

She finally finished.

They stared at each other.

"Samantha," he started.

She blew out a breath. "Just take me home."

He wished he could start over with a different song, but truthfully, all his songs were about Jamie. It was his one true heartbreak. But that was fifteen years ago. He'd seen Jamie at their ten-year high school reunion, and she was married with three kids. And hadn't that backfired on him, going into that reunion all hopeful and shit, thinking after all this time they might pick up where they'd left off. He pushed thoughts of Jamie away. That part of his life was done. And Samantha was the first woman he'd thought of as more than a quick lay in a very long time.

"Samantha, I'm sorry. It was just a song. Jamie doesn't mean anything to me anymore."

"Then why do you sing about her?"

He lifted one shoulder up and down.

How could he explain that he hadn't had any serious relationships since then? She'd think he was pathetic—hung up on the memory of his ex for years. Keeping things light and easy with the ladies was better than getting his heart broken. He figured she'd see that as a bad thing too, calling him a player, which he was. But somehow with Samantha he didn't want to be like that. He wanted to live up to her Prince Charming dreams. Maybe she could tell him how to fix it, the way she told him how to get closer to her in the first place.

Samantha shook her head in disgust.

"Is there anything I can do to fix tonight?" he asked. "Anything Prince Charming might do?"

"Why? So you can get me into bed?"

Yes!

The fire burning in her eyes made him hold his tongue. It

wasn't happening tonight.

"Come on," he said. "I'll take you home."

She grabbed her purse and coat and left. He followed her out and practically had to run to keep up with her.

He opened the truck door for her and couldn't help checking her out as she climbed in. He wanted her so bad he could taste it. Man, he'd really screwed up tonight. He should've insisted on meeting her mother on their first date. Then he would've known she was Mexican. Or he should've listened when his mother went on and on about the wonderful Dixon family and their perfect daughter Samantha. He hadn't thought it would matter back then. Now it did. A lot.

He had to write some songs not about Jamie and fast. Maybe something about the beautiful Samantha. He started the truck.

"And don't try any more of that Prince Charming stuff when we both know who you really are," she said in a choked voice.

"Samantha—"

"Just...don't."

He shut up. He knew he wasn't a prince, but damn if he didn't want to be for her.

~ ~ ~

That night, after he dropped off Samantha, Rico did something he'd never done before—he called his oldest sister, Maria, for woman advice. She was like a second mother, only much more in touch with the younger generation than his own mother.

"Hey, Maria," he said when she answered. "It's me."

"What's wrong?" Her concern made it easier for him to spill his guts. She always could read his moods.

The sad truth was he knew how to seduce a woman, but he had no clue what to do outside of the bedroom. His time with Jamie had been filled with her going to his varsity baseball games, his garage band rehearsals, his job at the mall. It struck him for the first time that Jamie had fit into his life with absolutely no effort on his part. No wonder he was clueless.

"I need some woman advice," he admitted.

"Ricky!" Maria exclaimed. "You finally met a special someone. Who's the lucky woman?"

He ground his teeth. He'd told everyone to call him Rico not Ricky way back when he was twelve. His sisters just loved to make him feel like the little baby bro. He was thirty-three, for crying out loud.

"Samantha," he said. The name rolled off his tongue. It was a beautiful name.

"Samantha. Now why does that name sound familiar?"

Probably because Samantha was all his mother could talk about for the rest of Thanksgiving. But he didn't want her putting two and two together and bringing their mother into his love life. Again.

"Don't know," he said. "So I found out she's really into, you know, romance." He searched for the right words. What had Samantha said when she was confessing her dreams to him? "A sweet romance like in the movies."

"And you have no clue."

"I have a clue. Just not the right one." He told her about the flowers and the ice-skating date that ended badly with the unfortunate miscommunication during his serenade.

"Wait a minute. Samantha was the one Mom set you up with. Of course she speaks Spanish, you moron!" He pulled the phone away from his ear at her volume. "Do you really think Mom's gonna set you up with someone that doesn't know how to speak Spanish to her grandbabies?"

That again? He wasn't looking to reproduce. He rubbed the back of his neck. He just wanted to look more like a prince in Samantha's eyes. Something about her made him want to try a little harder.

"So what do I do?" he asked.

"She wants a romance like in the movies, then you should watch some romantic movies."

"That's it? Just watch some movies?"

"Watch and learn, Ricky."

"Which ones?"

"Oh, there's so many. Did she say which movies are her favorites?"

His shoulders slumped. "No."

"All right. Start with *Pretty Woman*. Ooh, *When Harry Met Sally* is so good too and *Sleepless in Seattle*. That's a good start."

He grabbed a pen and scribbled the titles down on the back of a take-out menu. "Okay, thanks. I'll see if I can find them."

"Try streaming them or look on demand. They're mostly older movies. You should be able to get them. Call me if you have any questions."

He rolled his eyes. "I'm sure I won't have any questions."

"This is deep stuff. Give it some thought after you watch, okay?"

"All right, thanks."

"Good luck."

He hung up and found *Pretty Woman* on demand. He was fifteen minutes in and scratching his head. Was his sister crazy? This woman was a prostitute. How was this supposed to help him with Samantha?

His cell rang, and he grabbed it. "Rico."

"So you need love advice and you call Maria instead of me." It was his other sister, Elena.

"Uh…" He hit pause on the movie.

"You know she's been with Steve since high school. She knows *nothing*. I have experience."

"Okay, Miss Experience. Maria told me to watch *Pretty*

Woman, but this woman—"

"Figures. She told you all old movies, didn't she? Let me tell you what the *modern* woman wants."

Elena was only two years younger than Maria, but Elena always had a chip on her shoulder about who knew more about the important things in life.

"I'm listening," he said.

"Try watching *Juno, How to Lose a Guy in Ten Days*…are you writing this down?"

He grabbed a pen and scribbled quickly around the margins of the take-out menu. "Yeah. Wait. *Lose* a guy?"

"Trust me."

"If you say so." Women were a complete mystery, but he trusted her, so he went with it.

"*Say Anything*, that's the name of the movie," Elena went on. "It's old but a classic. *Lady and the Tramp.*"

"Isn't that a cartoon?"

"Then you should be able to understand it."

"Ouch."

"Sorry, little bro, but when it comes to women, you're still a beginner. I hope this woman helps you mature."

"I am mature!"

"Good luck, buddy."

She hung up, and he went back to *Pretty Woman*. He remained puzzled until the end when the guy climbed her fire escape, bearing roses and overcoming his fear of heights. That he could understand. It was like *Romeo and Juliet* plus bravery. He wrote that little gem down: climb fire escape with roses. He didn't have a fear of heights, but he could pretend.

He watched *Juno* next and wrote: fill mailbox with orange Tic Tacs.

By Sunday night, he'd watched all the recommended movies. From what he could tell, romance was like putting on a show. A performance in honor of the woman. And, it seemed, once you won them over, everything was golden.

He felt fully prepared to win Samantha over.

~ ~ ~

Samantha took her usual lunch break on Monday with a stop at the mailbox. She wondered if they'd start getting Christmas cards soon. It was only the first week of December, but there were always some early birds that whipped them out the day after Thanksgiving. She was still designing one for her family. Maybe she'd do a collage with the four seasons. She pulled open the mailbox, and an avalanche of orange Tic Tacs spilled out. "Ah!"

She jumped back in surprise. What the hell? How many little plastic boxes did it take to fill that mailbox? Who would do that? Was some teenager playing pranks in the neighborhood? She stared at the Tic Tacs all over what remained of the snow on the ground. She shook some off her boots and peeked into the mailbox. Was there any mail under there? There was a white envelope.

She pulled it out. No stamp. No return address. This was getting a little creepy. She looked up and down the street for any strange cars hovering nearby. Nothing out of the usual. Slowly, she opened the envelope and read the scrawled note.

Samantha,

Third time's the charm. Dinner Wednesday night? I'll pick you up at seven. Call me if you DON'T want to go. Sorry about that song. I'm working on a new one just for you.

Rico

Samantha stared at the note. He was writing a song just for her? No one had ever written her a song.

Still, she wasn't so sure a third date was a good idea. The other two had ended very badly. And nothing had changed, really. He was still a player.

She shook her head at the Tic Tac mess. She didn't even like orange Tic Tacs. She liked the white ones.

It was weird, she thought as she went inside for a bag to clean up the mess, but she had to give him points for originality.

Chapter Six

A dozen roses tucked inside his leather jacket, Rico hauled a ladder to the back of Samantha's house on Wednesday night. He was going to *Pretty Woman* her. She'd called and told him not to stop by, but had that stopped Romeo from visiting his Juliet? No, it had not. If there was one thing he'd learned from all those movies, it was that the guy didn't give up that easy.

Her parents didn't have a fire escape, but he thought the ladder should accomplish the same thing. He wasn't sure which bedroom was Samantha's. He saw a light on in one room and a shadow of someone moving around in there. Good enough.

Luckily most of the snow had melted from the couple of inches they'd gotten two days ago. He propped the ladder up, made sure it was stable, and began to climb. He wasn't afraid of heights like that guy in the movie, but maybe he could pretend he was to make it even more meaningful. He made it to the top and pulled the roses from his jacket.

Tap, tap, tap. He waited patiently for Samantha to answer his signal. He tapped again. The window shade flew up, and a petite Mexican woman appeared, took one look at him, and screamed bloody murder.

He startled and nearly lost his balance as the ladder wobbled. His heart raced. If he fell off this ladder, he'd likely end up in the hospital with multiple broken bones. The ladder steadied, and he tried to get her to stop screaming.

"It's Rico," he called through the window. "You know my mother."

She narrowed her eyes and slowly reached for something.

"It's Rico! *Mi madre es su amiga.*"

She got closer. *Mierda.* She had a wooden bat and looked like she was fully prepared to use it.

He tried again, yelling through the glass. "*Mi madre—*"

She pulled up the sash just a crack.

"Don't hurt me," he said. "It's Rico. You know my mother. *Mi madre—*"

"Rico del Toro?" she asked.

He blew out a breath of relief as the bat lowered. "Yes."

"What are you doing?"

"I'm being romantic. I thought this was Samantha's room."

A big grin split her face. "Don't go nowhere, Rico del Toro."

"Uh, okay." This was not going like in the movies.

A few minutes later, Samantha appeared with her mother at her side. His heart did a weird stutter.

"See?" her mother said, pointing at him. "Romantic."

Samantha rushed to the window. "What are you doing here? I told you not to come."

"Sam!" her mother chided.

"I'm overcoming my fear of heights to give you roses." He gestured for her to open the window more, and he slid them in.

Her eyebrows scrunched in confusion. "You didn't have to overcome your fear of heights for me."

Her mother tsked. "What do you say to the nice young man?"

"Thank you," Samantha said. Her brows furrowed, and

she just kept staring at him like he was crazy. Maybe he was.

"Come in through the front door," her mother said. "We've been wanting to meet you."

He nodded. Mission accomplished. He made his way down the ladder, glad he was getting the hang of this whole romance thing.

~ ~ ~

Samantha put the roses in a vase, musing over the fact that he'd given her roses twice now. It was so weird the way he showed up here tonight even after she left a message on his voice mail politely declining the dinner invitation. Had her mother put him up to this?

She peeked out the front window as he put the ladder in the back of his truck. They'd never even talked about his fear of heights before. It was kinda cool that he conquered his fear just to give her flowers.

He strutted up the front walk. The man did have confidence. She opened the door before he could knock.

He flashed a charming smile, and she felt an answering flutter low in her belly. The man was just too good at what he did—all those seductive smiles and deep gazes. When she made no move to invite him inside, merely stared at him, he spoke up.

"Your mother wanted to meet me."

"Oh, yeah. Come in." She turned and called toward the kitchen. "Ma-aa-aa, come meet Rico."

Her mother hurried to the foyer and immediately embraced him. She pulled back and smiled. "I'm Terisa Medina Dixon. You may call me Terisa."

Samantha's jaw dropped, and she stared at her mother. She always insisted on being called Mrs. Dixon as a sign of respect. What was it about Rico that she already had him on such familiar terms? Did she still think she'd arranged a marriage? *Please*.

Rico's smile lit up his face. He was absurdly handsome with his perfect white teeth and warm brown eyes that sorta sparkled. "Nice to meet you, Terisa. I'm Rico."

Her mother giggled. Giggled! Her mother never giggled. "Yes, yes, I know. Come meet my husband."

Rico followed her mother to the family room, where her father was watching the news.

"Lee!" her mother said sharply.

Her father jolted to attention and turned. "Oh, hey!" He stood and crossed the room to give Rico a hearty handshake. "You must be Rico. You're all I hear about around here."

Samantha's cheeks burned. It wasn't her doing all the talking about Rico.

"All good, I hope," Rico said, glancing at Samantha and giving her another gorgeous smile.

Her father slapped him on the back. "Of course, you're the chosen one."

"Da-aa-aad! Please." She turned to Rico. "This is my father, Lee."

Rico nodded. "Very nice to meet you, sir."

"Such nice manners," her mother crooned. "Have fun, you two!"

Samantha grabbed Rico's hand and pulled him out of the room. Her parents were so embarrassing. "Bye!"

"Boy, you're in a hurry to get me alone," Rico said.

She shook her head. "Why exactly are you here?"

"I'm here for you," he said simply.

"Rico, I appreciate the flowers, I really do, but if this is some weird thing between our mothers, don't worry about it. You've done your part. You're off the hook. Go find your next conquest."

He took her hand. His rough palm on hers sent tingles

straight up her arm. "I'm not looking for a conquest. If you'll just give me another chance, I'll prove it."

"Why?"

"Because you make me want to try harder. I want to be a prince for you."

Samantha felt herself weakening. That was really sweet. And he looked so sincere.

He kissed the back of her hand. "Please."

She took a deep breath and nodded.

He held her hand as they continued outside while Samantha marveled that she was actually going on a third date with Rico. She kept sneaking glances at him, still having trouble getting used to this new romantic side of him. She hadn't told him to do any of that stuff when she confessed her heartache to Santa that day. This must be what he was really like when he cared about a woman.

He opened the passenger-side door for her, waited for her to get in, and shut it. She glanced at the center console and saw a small spindly fern sitting in the cup holder.

He got in and picked up the plant. "This is for you. It's a love fern."

She stared at it. "A what?"

"You know, a love fern. It symbolizes the relationship."

"The relationship," she echoed. "Do we have a relationship?"

He leaned over and kissed her cheek. She warmed at the spot.

"It's symbolic," he said.

She stared at it, puzzled. First flowers, then a fern. "Uh, thank you."

"I'm taking you to a place with great fresh-made noodles. You like Chinese noodles?"

"Sure."

"Okay, then." He drove off, tapping his fingers on the

steering wheel in time to "Merry Christmas, Baby" by Bruce Springsteen.

Samantha relaxed into the seat, occasionally glancing at Rico and then at the fern. It was odd, but in a way beautiful. She felt herself softening toward him. It wasn't his fault they met through their crazy mothers. Maybe she'd been all wrong about him. Maybe he wasn't a player after all. Maybe he was just nervous the first couple of times she saw him, and now he was being himself. It was nice to be with a man that was honest after that two-faced liar Tim.

They arrived at the restaurant, and Rico helped her off with her coat. His warm hands brushed her shoulders, and she got a hot shiver. "You look beautiful tonight," he murmured near her ear.

"Thank you," she whispered.

He pulled out her chair for her. She was starting to get used to the gentlemanly manners. She could count on one hand the number of guys who'd ever bothered to do anything chivalrous like open her door or pull out her chair.

Rico opened the menu. "Let's share the Phoenix special. It says it's big enough for two."

She glanced at the menu. Noodles, veggies, and shrimp. "Sounds good to me."

Rico smiled at her, and she smiled back, basking in the sunshine of that smile.

"Rico, I appreciate everything you've done with the Tic Tacs and the roses and overcoming your fear of heights and the, um, love fern, but you don't have to do so much for me. I would've been happy with just a nice dinner."

"That's not what you told Santa," he teased.

She bit her lip. "That's just a fantasy. I know better."

He entwined his fingers with hers and gave her a hot look. "I want to make your fantasies come true."

A thrill ran through her. She had a feeling he could make

her fantasies come true in many interesting ways. It had been a long time, too long. "You're sweet."

He laughed. "No one has ever called me sweet."

"But you are!"

His thumb brushed back and forth over her palm. "So I'm not a player?"

"You tell me."

"I used to be. But you make me want more."

"I do?"

He smiled. "Yeah."

Their food arrived. A big pile of noodles.

Samantha lifted her fork. He stilled her hand. "Wait. Let's really share."

He lifted a noodle to her mouth and took the other end. A jolt of alarm ran through her. This was exactly like *Lady and the Tramp*. She'd watched it many times with her niece, Gabriella.

She pulled the noodle from her mouth. "That's *Lady and the Tramp*."

He sucked the noodle into his mouth. "Romantic, right?"

She rubbed her temple. All the things he'd done tonight had been so strange. Were they all from movies? Her previous elation over his gestures deflated. Was he still playing her?

"Where did you get the idea for a love fern?" she asked.

"It's just a gesture. You know, romance. *How to Lose a Guy*."

Her brows scrunched together. "Lose a guy?"

"I know it sounds weird. But it was a romantic movie by the end."

"I don't know that one." She was getting a really bad feeling. "The roses on a ladder? Was that *Romeo and Juliet*?"

"Classic, yeah. Also in *Pretty Woman*."

"Are you really afraid of heights?" Her voice rose in volume, but she couldn't help it. She was starting to feel like a fool, falling for what amounted to a bag of tricks he stole from movies.

"Not anymore," he said.

She shook her head. "Orange Tic Tacs?" She slapped her forehead. "I remember now. That was from *Juno*. Was anything that happened here tonight really you?"

"Sure."

"Which part?"

"I really do like noodles."

Her head ached and her heart too. This was so disappointing. She'd actually thought she was seeing the real Rico when it was all just a big phony act.

"Rico, this is just too weird. I want to go home."

"But we just started eating."

"I'll wait in the truck." She got up and left, walking quickly to the exit. She didn't care that it was freezing cold out. She was beginning to think that her first impression was right. He *was* a player. He was playing at romance to get her into bed. Here she'd thought he was being genuine. Yes, she wanted romance, but only if that person was romantic because they truly felt something for her. Even more importantly, she wanted someone that was honest with her.

She turned just as Rico came barreling toward her running full steam. He looked nuts. She started to back away, moving to the other side of the truck. He changed directions and headed straight for her. She squeaked and ran.

He caught her with a quick grab, turned her to face him, and set his hands on her shoulders, anchoring her in place. He panted. "I saw that in *When Harry Met Sally*. He runs to her. At least you made that one easy for me."

"Omigod. Are you going to hold up a boom box tonight in my backyard, playing our song?"

He nodded sagely. "*Say Anything*. They don't make those anymore. I checked."

She stared at him, incredulous.

"I could hold up an iPod," he offered. When she just stared at him, he added, "We could still meet at the top of the Empire State building."

Sleepless in Seattle.

"What is wrong with you?" she asked in complete exasperation. "Can't you just be yourself?"

She hugged herself, feeling like an absolute fool that she'd been taken in by all those lies. He studied her for a moment, and his hands loosened on her shoulders. Good. She just wanted all this weird stuff to—

Suddenly she was flush against his body as one hand pressed the small of her back, the other cupped the back of her head. The kiss was raw and carnal, his mouth claiming hers, his tongue thrusting inside, and heat rushed through her. His stubble scraped her lightly, and her knees went weak. Lord, he was a good kisser. His leg wedged between hers, and she throbbed for him. The kiss went on and on, the delicious friction of his leg between hers had her insides spiraling and tightening. Omigod, she was gonna—

He pulled back, easing his leg from between hers, and looked into her eyes. "That was me."

Words failed her. She nodded.

Then he kissed her again, and that marvelous leg was back. His hands slid to her bottom, rocking her, and the spiraling started again, sensation after sensation, all centered on that one spot he'd managed to reach through her jeans. She moaned, not even caring they were in a parking lot. He was like a drug and she couldn't get enough. Her hands fisted on the back of his shirt, keeping him close, never wanting the kiss to end.

"Hey, Rico," a woman's voice called.

Rico broke the kiss, releasing his hold on Samantha to look over at a beautiful redhead showing a lot of leg in a miniscule skirt and heels that were entirely inappropriate for December in Connecticut.

"Looks like the noodle date's working out for you," the redhead called with a smirk.

"Get lost, Jolene," Rico called back with good humor.

Samantha staggered back. Her legs felt like jelly. She still throbbed, hot and wet with need. But she was just one of many to him.

"This is just part of some typical date routine, isn't it?" Samantha asked. "God, I'm such a fool."

"No! I mean I've been here before with a date but—"

"Home."

She went to the passenger side of the truck and waited for him to unlock it. He exhaled sharply and then opened her door.

"Samantha, you're not like girls like Jolene—"

"Save it. I don't need any pretty words or fake romance. Just save it." She blinked back tears. She couldn't believe she'd been taken in by…she'd almost…just from a kiss.

She was a fool.

He gently shut her door, and she rested her forehead against the cool window.

She wished she'd never met Rico del Toro.

Chapter Seven

Rico hadn't been to the doctor for a physical in years. He'd called for a checkup when he got those weird heart palpitations. He was getting them on a more regular basis, and they were scaring the shit out of him.

Dr. Amoretto went through the usual listen-and-look stuff and seemed pretty casual when he wrote stuff in Rico's chart. Not like he thought Rico might keel over at any minute. Rico couldn't take the suspense anymore.

"So am I okay, doc?"

Dr. Amoretto paused in his note taking. "You appear to be a healthy thirty-three-year-old man."

"Good. Okay."

The doc scribbled something else and looked up. "Your blood work will be back in a few days, but I don't anticipate any issues."

Rico nodded.

The doc set his pen down. "Anything else you'd like to talk about today?"

Rico tensed. Should he mention his heart? It hadn't bothered him all day. On the other hand, it was the whole reason he'd made the appointment. He probably wouldn't be back for a while.

Rico stared at the menorah sitting next to a small artificial

Christmas tree on the counter. "There is one thing," he said slowly.

"What is it?"

Rico rubbed his chest and faced the doctor, who peered at him, all business. "I've been getting these weird heart palpitations. Kind of painful."

The doctor raised his pen. "Can you describe the pain?"

"It's like it skips a beat. Sometimes it squeezes or, I dunno, like, flip-flops."

Dr. Amoretto stood, put his stethoscope back in his ears, and listened to Rico's heart again. A few minutes later, he pulled the stethoscope out of his ears. "Sounds okay to me. What were you doing when it happened?"

Rico shrugged. "Last time I was on a date, just standing in a parking lot."

"And the other times?"

Rico thought about that. "One time was at her house. Once in the truck."

The corner of the doc's mouth pulled up. "Were you with the same woman in the truck?"

"Yeah." He'd been with Samantha, but what did that have to do with anything?

The doc crossed his arms and grinned. "In my professional opinion, you're in love."

Rico broke out in a cold sweat despite the fact he always ran hot. Say what?

"Or lust," the doc went on. "One or the other. It's definitely the woman."

He'd been in lust plenty of times without any of this heart weirdness.

It hit him like a slap to the face, left him shocked and stinging, because the last time he'd seen Samantha she'd wanted nothing to do with him. He was in love? He hadn't felt like this at all with Jamie. She had been familiar, warm, uncomplicated. Samantha was like a jolt to his system. A damn wake-up call to his life. This must be the kind of love that made Trav trail Daisy around like a pathetic lost puppy. He'd laughed at Trav. He wasn't laughing now.

He had to get Samantha back.

~ ~ ~

Samantha worked on her latest freelance assignment—a book cover for a best-selling unicorn fantasy series—and found herself adding stubble to the unicorn's cheeks, thinking of Rico's perpetual stubble. What was wrong with her? When Rico dropped her off two days ago after that very weird showboating date, she'd been sure meeting him was the worst thing to ever happen to her but now…She kept replaying their kiss. Her almost…kiss-gasm. She'd never had one of those.

Of course he was a good kisser; he had plenty of practice.

He was trying too hard.

Still, it was kinda nice to have a guy actually try to impress her. Even if it was misguided and strange and fake.

She picked up her cell to call her sister, Lucia, the only person on the planet she could tell about the man their mother had chosen for her arranged marriage. She shook her head. The entire time with Rico was utterly ridiculous—an arranged marriage, a setup from their mothers. I mean, please! Like any good romance ever started out *that* way.

She dialed Lucia.

"What?" her sister said.

"Um, hello? It's Sam."

"I've got dinner about to burn, and Gabriella is using the furniture as her own personal—" Her voice called to the other room. "Stop jumping! I do not need another trip to the emergency room! Santa is watching you!" She returned to the phone. "I need a break. You up for a late night Christmas shopping run once Joe gets home?"

"Sure."

"Okay, bye."

Samantha went back to her unicorn, erasing the stubble. It was just as ridiculous as the rest of her life.

~ ~ ~

That night Samantha braved the Mega Toy Crazy store with her sister.

"It's a special two-hour sale," Lucia said as she maneuvered into a parking space. "Come on! Our mission is Violet. I heard they just got a fresh stock of them."

Lucia leaped out of the car, surprisingly agile for a pregnant woman battling morning sickness, and was already halfway to the entrance when Samantha broke into a run to catch up to her.

So much for a sisterly heart-to-heart about men, Samantha thought wryly. Lucia had vented the entire drive about her pregnancy fatigue and nausea, and how she was sure Gabriella was acting out because she knew she wasn't going to be number one anymore.

She followed Lucia to where a mob was swarming the doll section. Samantha stayed back. The fluorescent lights overhead combined with the crowd and "Feliz Navidad" blasting over the speakers made her want to run screaming out of the store. What in the world was so great about a Violet doll? She waited while the voices rose and fell as people jostled each other to get the coveted doll. A few people emerged triumphant, and then Lucia appeared, Violet doll hugged close, guarding against a possible dollnapping from another insanely eager parent.

Lucia beamed. "I got it!"

The doll wore a violet dress, violet shoes, and had huge violet eyes. Kinda creepy, actually. At least her hair was brown, not violet.

"What's so special about…" Samantha's voice died in her throat. Rico was heading right for her, Violet doll tucked under one arm like a football. "It's him," she said under her breath to Lucia.

"Him who?" Lucia asked loudly.

"Hey," Rico said, stopping in front of her. He smelled like musk and leather, and her knees weakened.

"Hey," Samantha croaked. She cleared her throat. "This is my sister, Lucia. Lucia, Rico."

Rico shook her hand. "Nice to meet you. Looks like we both came out victorious."

"It was close." Lucia grinned. "Luckily I elbowed my way in there."

"Why are you buying a Violet doll?" Samantha asked Rico.

Was this another one of his strange things? Had he followed her here because of some movie? A chill ran down her spine. Was he a stalker?

Rico smiled sheepishly. "My sister asked me to get it for my niece Sophia. They're sold out in Florida."

"Oh."

They stared at each other, right there in the middle of Mega Toy Crazy, with parents buzzing all around. *You can't win me over*, she told him telepathically. *No matter how good a kisser you are.*

"I'll, just, ah, do a little shopping," Lucia said, scampering off. She called over her shoulder, "Meet me at the register!"

"Okay," Samantha called.

"Samantha," Rico said.

The way he said her name sounded like a melody. Most people called her plain old Sam.

"What?" she asked, reaching for strength against his obvious charms. This was exactly why he was a player. Women fell for that stuff. She was stronger than that.

He took her hand and pulled her away from the crowd. He looked so strange in this environment with his black leather jacket and worn jeans like a motorcycle-riding badass. Behind him were pink and sparkly princess dress-up clothes.

"I meant what I said the other night," he said urgently. "You're not like those other girls, like Jolene, just out for a good time. That's what makes you special."

"But what about you? You are like them, out for a good time. Aren't you? If your mother hadn't set it up, you never would have asked someone like me out."

"No, but—"

"I don't want to be one of your long list of conquests."

"I don't keep a list," he said with a quick grin. He tapped his head. "It's all up here."

Exactly. Samantha wasn't looking for a quickie. She wanted a real relationship with someone who truly cared about her. Someone that wasn't putting on an act.

"Good-bye, Rico." She caught his frown before she turned and hurried to meet up with her sister.

She found Lucia near the end of a long line.

"Everything okay?" Lucia asked.

"Fine," Samantha said.

Lucia raised a brow. "Who was that?"

Samantha leaned close to whisper in Lucia's ear. "The guy Mom set me up with."

Lucia's jaw dropped. "He's gorgeous! I can't believe that's who Mom set you up with. He looks like a sex god." She fanned herself. "I should've let Mom set me up with someone when she tried years ago."

"He's an immature, womanizing beast," Samantha replied as calmly as she could. She caught a black leather jacket out of the corner of her eye as Rico walked by on his way to another long line. She stiffened and looked only at Lucia.

"There he is!" Lucia exclaimed. She waved. Rico waved

back.

Samantha's cheeks burned. "Just ignore him."

"Are you going to go out with him again?" Lucia asked out of the corner of her mouth, still stealing glances at Rico.

"No. And stop looking at him!" she hissed. "Don't give him any attention."

"Are you nuts?" Lucia asked, fanning herself again.

Samantha grabbed Lucia's fanning hand. "Stop it. He can see you."

Lucia gave her a pointed look. "I'm married and pregnant and even I want him. Of course he's a beast. He probably has to beat women off with a stick."

Samantha raised her chin. "Not this woman."

"If only..." her sister muttered, gazing appreciatively over at Rico.

Samantha looked over. Rico raised a hand in greeting. She faced front, ignoring her full-body blush, and prayed he couldn't see it from across the store.

Chapter Eight

Rico got back to his apartment with the Violet doll, feeling lower than a stray dog. Why did he have to fall in love with Samantha, who clearly wanted nothing to do with him? They'd had three dates, all of which ended badly, and she seemed immune to his usual charm. Most women he would've slept with already. First, second date tops. It really seemed to bug her that he had experience. She should be glad. That meant he knew what he was doing.

He set the doll in the bedroom closet, unwilling to have the creepy huge purple eyes of Violet follow him around all weekend. He'd mail it out on Monday. He headed to the kitchen for a beer. Normally he'd go to the bar on a Friday night and pick up someone, but that was ruined now that he'd fallen in love. *Thanks a lot, Ma. You sure can pick 'em.* It was the ultimate payback for all his slutting around. The irony was not lost on him.

He popped open the cap and took a long drink. He should call Elena and let her know he got the doll. He pulled out his cell and punched in her number.

When she answered, he surprised even himself when he blurted, "The doc says I'm in love."

"Rico?"

"Yeah."

"Did you get Violet?"

"Yes, I got the doll. Did you hear me?"

"I heard you, but you're not making any sense. The doctor said you're in love. Are you seeing a shrink?"

"No." He blew out a breath. "I thought I had a heart condition, so I went for a physical. The doc says my heart's fine and—"

"You're in love."

"I need advice. She wants nothing to do with me." Then to butter her up, he added, "I'm asking you first."

"Hmph. You should always come to me first. Is it Samantha?"

"Yeah."

"She didn't go for your romantic date? What'd you end up doing, anyway?"

"I don't want to talk about it."

"How can I help you if you won't tell me what you did wrong?"

He started pacing. "I didn't do anything wrong! I did everything the guys did in the movies!"

"Everything?"

"Yes!"

"Hmmm…"

He stopped pacing and blew out a breath. "She keeps harping on the fact that I've been with other women. Why does that even matter? I'm sure she's been with other men. God, I hope so."

He shuddered. He didn't want to break in a thirty-year-old virgin. Way too much pressure for a guy.

"What exactly did she say?" Elena asked.

He stared at the beer in his hand, thinking hard. "I dunno. Something about being part of my long list of conquests."

"Did you brag about other women?"

"No! I know better than that. I mean we ran into Jolene,

and there was that song about Jamie—"

"All right, little bro, I got this. It's simple. She wants to feel special."

"I told her she was special."

"That's not enough. Okay, here's what you gotta do."

Rico listened, feeling a little queasy, then quickly got off the phone. Was he really going to do this? Could he bear to go through with it?

~ ~ ~

The next morning Rico showed up at Book It the moment they opened. He wanted to be the first one at the bookstore— in and out with no witnesses. The owner, Rachel Miller, who also co-owned Something's Brewing Café with Shane, flipped the sign to open and let him in.

"Good morning, Rico," she said. "I haven't seen you here before. Is there something I can help you find?"

His eyes darted around the store. "Just browsing."

She gestured inside. "Enjoy."

He cruised up and down the aisles, scanning the labels on the shelves. History, Biography, Sports. No, no, no. He kept going. Kids section. He grabbed several picture books for his youngest niece and some adventure novels for the older nieces and nephews. It was a good cover for his real mission anyway. He kept going. Cookbooks, Hobbies, Mystery. And then he found it. The label for the large section was in purple script: Romance.

The bell jingled on the front door, and he quickly moved back to the mystery section. He picked up a book and watched as an older woman approached. She went straight to romance and picked out a book. He glanced over. It was in the New Releases section. She went to the register. He snatched a copy of that same book and hid it behind the mystery in his hand.

The books were becoming unwieldy. He needed a basket or something. He set the stack of books on the floor and pretended to be checking out the mysteries while he listened to Rachel chatting with her customer and ringing up the purchase. Finally the woman left.

Rico took one of each on the New Releases shelf, bringing his total to a dozen romance books. *Elena better know what she's talking about*, he thought grimly. He balanced the romances under one arm and bent to scoop up the stack of books he'd left on the floor.

Crash! The books scattered everywhere.

Rachel appeared in front of him and took in all the books, her eyes lingering on the romances. "Oh my."

"It's for my sister!" he exclaimed.

She bent down and started gathering books. "Sure, sure. No problem. She might like the latest from Lorelai White too."

"Okay, I'll try that—I mean, take that one. It's Christmas, after all."

She grinned.

He avoided her eyes and quickly grabbed all the other books. He followed her to the register.

"You really want all these other books or are they just a cover?" Rachel asked. She looked like she was trying not to laugh.

Rico cringed. "I told you I'm Christmas shopping. I need everything."

The bell jingled again, and Barry, the guy who played elf to his Santa, walked in.

"The picture books alone will run you a hundred bucks," Rachel said.

Barry stopped at Biographies.

"Yes, yes, hurry!" Rico slapped his credit card on the counter.

Rachel giggled and started ringing them up. Rico kept his

back to Barry, who had moved to Personal Growth. Was Rachel going extra slow on purpose? Sweat broke out on his forehead. Barry was a loudmouth. He did *not* want this getting around Clover Park.

He should've just bought this stuff online, but he wanted to get started on his research right away. He ducked down, rubbing the back of his neck.

"Hey, Rachel!" Barry called.

"Hey, Barry," Rachel said. "Can I help you find anything?"

Suddenly Barry was at his side. "Hey, I know you! Santa, right?"

Rico grimaced. There were still two books to go, both of which featured a bare-chested man about to kiss a woman who appeared close to orgasm. He had to distract him. He shifted, blocking Barry's view. "Yup, that was me. Good to see you. How's the fro-yo business?"

"Wonderful! I just got a few new flavors for the holidays: candy cane, cinnamon swirl, and gingerbread."

Rico smiled tightly. "Great. That sounds great."

Barry peeked over his shoulder. "Ooh, *Carnal Werewolf.* That's a good one."

Rico's eyes widened.

Barry shrugged. "My mom leaves them lying around."

He lived with his mother? He was in his thirties. And he openly admitted to reading these girly books?

Rachel finally finished ringing him up and slid the books into a brown bag, a small smile playing on her lips.

"It's for my sister," he insisted. He signed the credit card slip and bolted out of the store.

~ ~ ~

Rico emptied the bag of books on the coffee table and stared at them. Was he really going to read romance novels? His sister was probably laughing her head off at the stupid advice she'd given him. His leg jiggled nervously. What was the big deal? It was just a book. He was alone. He'd already done the hard part, buying them. His leg jiggled again.

He stood abruptly and got a drink of water. He could do this. Sure, he wasn't much of a reader, except for the sports section of the paper, but Elena said it would make everything clear for him. He *was* confused. He really wanted to figure this thing out. Not just to sleep with Samantha, though he did want her in his bed. If he was in love, he wanted to be with that person. He wanted Samantha to think better of him. He wanted to be better.

He finished his water in one long swallow, set the glass in the sink, and marched determinedly over to the table. He stuck the gift books back in the bag and lined up the romances across the table, unsure where to begin. A lot of half-naked men here. He got up and slid the deadbolt on his front door.

He grabbed *Blazing Embrace* and began to read. Okay, no big deal. The guy was some billionaire industry tycoon. Must be nice. The woman was applying for a job as the new CFO. Hey, now, this woman was already hot for the guy. He kept going.

Three hours later, he wiped a tear from his eye, glad he was alone. It was so fucking beautiful at the end when they finally got together. He just knew Cole and Mia were gonna make it. A real happy-ever-after. He sniffled and picked up the next book in the pile, *Highlander's Mission*. The guy wore a kilt. He had no idea how this one might help him. Ooh, it started out with a battle. Nice. He kept going.

Three hours later, throat tight, he closed the book. He took a deep, satisfied breath. Roan and Brianna were perfect for each other. He grabbed a bag of chips and a beer and dove into *Carnal Werewolf*. He shifted uncomfortably as the opening scene began doggie-style. He couldn't take much more of these sex scenes without some relief. Damn, it was hot in here. He went for a shower to take care of business before he got blue balls, and went right back to reading.

By the end of the weekend, he felt calm, satisfied due to numerous showers, and confident he'd gleaned a key insight into the female psyche. Elena was brilliant. He finally understood what women wanted both physically and emotionally. The men took charge in the bedroom. He already did that, but he could up his game. They went down on the woman a lot. Well, duh, of course women liked that. He usually received that pleasure, but with Samantha he really wanted to give. They also talked a lot about emotions. He wasn't so good at that. He could steal a line or two from the billionaire or maybe the laird. He flipped through the books and took some notes.

Samantha hadn't liked the moves he'd pulled from the movies, but this was different. This was gold. Like the keys to the kingdom—a clear vision of the female mind. There was no way she could resist someone that understood her as he now did.

So at seven o'clock on Sunday night, he dressed in a shirt he left half unbuttoned to show off more chest like the men on the book covers, and drove to Samantha's house.

Chapter Nine

Samantha was helping clear the dinner dishes on Sunday night when the doorbell rang.

"Could you get that, *mija*?" her mother asked.

She set the plates in the sink. "Sure."

She headed to the door and peeked through the peephole. Rico!

What was he doing here? She'd thought she'd been pretty clear she didn't want someone like him in her life.

Just open the door. See what he wants.

She opened the door, and her jaw dropped. He wasn't wearing a jacket, and his white shirt was half unbuttoned, revealing a golden, muscular chest with pecs and six-pack abs. She'd never seen such a beautiful man in real life, only in the movies or on the covers of her favorite novels.

"You must be freezing!" she exclaimed, tearing her eyes away from his swoon-worthy chest. "Come in."

He stepped inside.

"Who is it?" her mother asked, coming out of the kitchen to see.

"It's Rico," Samantha said.

"Hello, Mrs. Dixon," Rico said.

"Oh!" Her mother giggled. "Just call me Terisa. I'll leave you sweethearts alone."

"We're not sweethearts, Ma!" Samantha called over her shoulder. She turned to Rico. "So…"

"Can we talk?" he asked.

"Uh, sure." She gestured for him to follow her to the formal living room. No one ever went in there, so it was sure to be private. The room was all white—white sofa, white chairs, and white carpet that still had the vacuum lines on it in perfect symmetry. She sat on the sofa, and he sat next to her.

"What did you want to talk about?" Samantha asked.

"I'm a strong man, and I need a strong woman at my side," he said.

Her brows scrunched in confusion. Was this part of the arranged marriage deal? Did her mother tell him to say that? It sounded so formal.

At her silence, he went on. "I don't know what love is, but I had a glimpse of it once, and…I just want to get to know you, and I want you to get to know me."

She opened her mouth to ask him if her mother had put him up to this, but he covered her mouth with his fingertips and gazed into her eyes. "Yes, I've been with other women, but I've thought of nothing but you since the day we met."

She blinked. "Really?" she asked around his fingertips.

He dropped his hand. "Really. And I'm not just trying to get you into bed, though that would be great. I want both the physical and emotional side."

She had to admit he was getting to her. He just kept trying so hard. She had to give him some credit for that. "Rico, that's really nice—"

Her words were lost as he gripped her hair and his mouth crashed down over hers. She tasted passion like she'd never felt before. It was exhilarating and exciting like she'd always dreamed about. She roamed her hands over his overheated beautiful chest as his kiss stole her breath away.

The phone rang nearby, and she reluctantly pulled away as

reality seeped back in.

He stroked her cheek. "My family is scattered around the country, but I want you to meet my second family so you can get to know me. They're having a tree-decorating party on Friday night. Can you go?"

She smiled. This was what she really wanted. Getting to know each other. And his words tonight. They were so heartfelt. So powerful. So honest. "I'd love to."

~ ~ ~

Rico stood with Samantha on the front porch of Maggie O'Hare's house on Friday night for the tree-decorating party. They could already hear loud voices inside and some really awful Christmas carols blaring that sounded like they were sung by chipmunks.

He turned to Samantha. He should warn her. "So I told you how Trav's like a brother and his grandmother's like a second mother to both of us, but I left out something. Maggie can be a little out there, but you know, whatever she does…she means well."

"Oh-kay."

He nodded once and knocked on the door.

A few minutes later, it swung open. Maggie stood there wearing a Santa hat with mistletoe dangling on the pom-pom right over her forehead and a red velvet jumpsuit with a black sash. Surprisingly, she held a Chihuahua wearing a tiny headband with mistletoe that stuck straight up from the center. A tiny red bow wrapped around the top of the mistletoe.

"Welcome, welcome!" Maggie kissed Rico's cheek and turned to Samantha. "So nice to meet you finally, Samantha. I've heard all about you from your mother."

Rico stared at her in alarm. Maggie was in on that too?

"You know my mother?" Samantha asked. She looked as

shocked as he felt.

Maggie nodded. "We met at Jorge's dance studio. She's a beauty on the dance floor." The mistletoe on her hat bobbed as she talked. "Come on in. We're just getting started."

Rico stepped inside as the pieces fell in place in his mind. Maggie had talked to Mrs. Dixon, and he already knew she chatted with his mother regularly. Then he remembered when he'd played Santa, Maggie had sat on his lap and told him, "You're next on my love-match list." Maggie had brought him and Samantha together.

Rico leaned down to whisper in Maggie's ear, "Thank you."

She grinned and whispered back, "Harold was in on it too."

His mind reeled. Maggie was the reason he'd suffered through three hours in the red suit? He glanced over at Samantha. Ah, it was worth it.

"Eggnog?" Maggie asked loudly over the music.

"No, thanks," Rico said. He couldn't help smiling. This crazy, meddling woman brought him Samantha.

"I'm fine," Samantha said.

It smelled so good in here, like fresh pine, cinnamon, and gingerbread. A Christmas tree stood in one corner of the living room. Trav's brother Shane must be baking something good in the kitchen. He was a chef. A fire crackled in the fireplace. The mantel was covered with greenery and pine cones with silver glitter. Red stockings embroidered "Maggie" and "Jorge" hung from the mantel.

"Who's that?" Rico asked loudly, pointing to the dog.

"Oh! This is Jorge's early Christmas present!" Maggie hollered over the music. "Say hello to Rice and Beans."

"Long name," Rico hollered back.

The music suddenly quieted, and Maggie turned. Her husband of one year, Jorge, approached. "The kids said it was too loud," Jorge said.

"It's a classic," Maggie said indignantly just as the chipmunks hit a high note wishing them a merry Christmas.

Jorge smiled and gazed into Maggie's eyes. "Mistletoe."

They kissed.

Rico and Samantha exchanged a look. It was sweet.

"How did you pick Rice and Beans for a name?" Samantha asked.

"Maggie knows she's the rice to my beans," Jorge said. "So he's Rice and Beans." He turned to Samantha, took her hand, and kissed it. Samantha blushed prettily. "Welcome, Samantha, I am Jorge."

"Thank you," Samantha said.

"We call him RB for short," Maggie said. The bobbing mistletoe was a little distracting. "Aren't you a happy dog, RB?"

RB looked with soulful eyes up at Maggie as if to say, *Why am I wearing this damn headband? I look like a dork.*

Maggie scratched RB behind the ear. "He's a senior citizen. We got him at seniors-for-seniors day at the shelter."

"Hey, you made it," Trav said, coming over to greet them.

"Trav, I want you to meet Samantha." Rico suddenly felt like this was a momentous occasion, introducing his love to his best friend. "Samantha, Travis O'Hare."

"Very nice to meet you, Samantha," Trav said. "You let me know if this guy gives you any trouble. I'll put him in his place."

Rico resisted the usual punch to Trav's arm he would've done at that remark. He really wanted to make a good impression on Samantha now that he had a third, no, fourth chance. Geez, this was probably his last chance. He wanted to be that mature guy.

Trav looked at Rico strangely.

"I'm sure that won't be necessary," Samantha said.

Trav's wife, Daisy; Ryan's wife, Liz; and Shane's soon-to-be wife, Rachel (from the bookstore), came over to meet Samantha. While the ladies talked, Rico said hello to Trav's brothers, Ryan and Shane. Trav's son, Bryce, ran by, squeaking a blue bone dog toy.

Ryan and Shane headed to the basement and returned carrying stacks of boxes marked Xmas Stuff. They set them on the coffee table.

Maggie rubbed her hands together. "Lights first, that's Ryan's job. Trav, you've got garland. Shane, you're the star." None of the brothers complained. It was tradition for them to do those jobs every year. "Everyone else can put up whatever ornaments they want wherever they want. Just keep the fragile ones up high away from Bryce's grabbing hands."

Ryan went over to do the lights while the rest of them sat around talking and snacking on a platter of crackers, cheese, and grapes.

Bryce ran over to Samantha and grabbed her leg.

She squatted down to his level. "Hello, Bryce. What do you got there?"

Bryce opened his bright blue eyes wide and stared at her. Probably dazzled by her beauty just like Rico was. He handed her the dog bone.

"Thank you!" Samantha exclaimed, holding the bone, which was still shiny with dog drool.

Something in Rico's chest ached again. He rubbed his chest. He had to nail this love thing down before he keeled over from heart failure.

Shane set down a platter of what were no doubt fresh-baked gingerbread cookies. Rico helped himself to a gingerbread girl wearing a busty dress. Only Maggie would decorate a cookie like that.

A short while later, Rico relaxed as Samantha seemed to be having a good time chatting with everyone. He stayed by her side, refilling her water glass whenever it got low. He was glad she was getting along with everyone.

"Time to decorate!" Maggie exclaimed. "Have at it!"

Everyone crowded around the newly opened ornament boxes. Trav handed Bryce a wooden teddy bear to hang on the tree that said, "Baby's First Christmas." It must have been from last year. Rico's throat got tight. Geez, ever since he read those romance novels he was so damn emotional. Those things were dangerous.

Everyone was talking and laughing and teasing each other, but Rico didn't join in. He remained quiet, watching Samantha decorate. Watching her smile. His chest aching even more.

Maggie walked by and plopped the Santa hat with mistletoe on his head. "Looks like you could use this more than me," she said with a wink.

"That's okay," he said. "You keep it."

The room went silent. Everyone stared at him. He held his hands up. "I'm not putting on a show here."

Trav looked at him with some concern. "Hey, you feeling okay?"

"Yeah, I'm fine." But he wasn't fine. He felt like he was having an out-of-body experience, floating on the outside, dreamy and lost on the inside. He shook his head. "I'm fine."

They went back to decorating. Rico stood at Samantha's side. The little dog settled under the tree and stared at Rico, that damn mistletoe sticking straight up off his head like a signal directed right at him.

He fetched some more water for him and Samantha, needing to cool off. He couldn't very well kiss Samantha the way he wanted to in front of this crowd. He returned to her side.

"Are you having fun?" he asked.

She beamed at him, and his heart did another flip-flop. "Yes! Thanks so much for inviting me."

Unable to resist any longer, he pulled her close and gave her a quick kiss.

"See, he didn't need mistletoe," Trav said.

Samantha blushed, and he felt his own cheeks burn. Since when did Trav ever get to him? He shot his friend a death look.

Trav laughed and laughed.

Rico shifted to the other side of Samantha, away from Trav. Rachel was there hanging candy canes.

"A new Susanna Potter came in you might like," Rachel whispered. "Should I put it on hold for you?"

He nodded once, his cheeks burning again. Susanna Potter wrote the romance *Once More, My Sweet* that had him choking back tears at the end. When Alex came out of his coma and his first words were "once more, my sweet Tatiana," he had to put the book down to get a hold of himself. Those romance novels had opened up something inside of him, some well of emotion that he couldn't push back down. He turned to Samantha, suddenly wanting her all to himself.

"You want to go Christmas shopping with me tomorrow?" he asked.

She smiled. "Sure."

"We'll make a day of it."

"Sounds fun."

He kissed her cheek, and something in him relaxed. He'd have her alone. Shopping, the best hot chocolate in town at Shane and Rachel's café, and back to his place. He'd have her all to himself, in his arms, and in his bed, where he absolutely knew she belonged.

After the tree was decorated, Shane and Maggie went to the kitchen to warm up food for everyone. A short while later, they gathered around the dining room table set up like a buffet and filled their plates with bite-size appetizers—tiny little crab puffs, shrimp wrapped in bacon, spanokopita, pigs in blankets, and bruschetta. He eyed the desserts sitting on platters on a sideboard. Peppermint fudge pie, apple pie—that explained the cinnamon he'd been smelling the whole night—chocolate mini-cupcakes, and cheesecake with crushed candy cane on top.

Rachel suddenly ran from the room, hand covering her mouth.

Shane jumped up and followed her. "Rach, you okay?" he called.

Maggie beamed. "Merry Christmas to me!" She turned to Rico. "Thank you, Santa!"

Realization dawned as Rico remembered Maggie's wish for more great-grandbabies.

"Shane doesn't know, does he?" Maggie asked. "I'll keep my mouth shut."

"Know what?" Trav asked.

"It's either the flu or she's pregnant," Daisy said. "She seemed fine earlier. I'd say she's pregnant."

Liz and Ryan smiled at each other.

Trav's jaw dropped. "Already?"

"It only takes once," Daisy replied with a significant look. "Shh-shh."

Shane came back in, looking very worried. He sank into a chair.

"Everything okay?" Maggie asked.

"Rachel's sick." Shane's brows scrunched. "Maybe I should take her home."

Everyone looked at each other, smiling.

"What?" Shane asked.

"Shall we eat?" Maggie asked.

Everyone dug into the delicious food. Rachel returned and sat down.

"Should I take you home?" Shane asked, all concern.

"No, I'm fine," Rachel said.

Shane set a plate of food in front of her. "Sure?"

"Yeah, something didn't settle with..." She took one look at the food, clapped a hand over her mouth, and ran from the room.

Shane jumped up and followed her. A moment later, they heard Rachel yell, "Go away!"

Shane returned to the table, his face grim. "I'm taking her home."

"You do that, love," Maggie said. "Take good care of our girl."

Samantha looked at Rico and smiled. He smiled back, getting more used to the heart squeeze at her beautiful smile. It was kinda funny how clueless Shane was. His sisters had been the same way in the first trimester—nauseous, exhausted, snarling at their husbands. He wondered if Samantha would be that way, and had a vision of her pregnant, round with his child. He stopped smiling. He had a long road ahead to get her there.

The Chihuahua took a seat in the corner of the room and stared at Rico again. That damn mistletoe on RB's head taunted him, daring him to kiss Samantha again.

I will! He silently told the little ancient dog. *Just not now. When I take her home.*

Rachel returned again. "Sorry. I'm, uh, not hungry. I'll just hang out by the tree."

Shane stood. "We're going home."

"I just need to rest a bit," Rachel insisted. "I'm fine."

He crossed to her and murmured something close to her ear. She looked to the ceiling, obviously annoyed.

"Don't make a big deal," Rachel said.

She headed into the living room, Shane on her heels. A few minutes later, they heard a squeal and the front door opening.

"Bye, all!" Shane called.

"Bye!" they chorused.

"Shane's in for a treat," Maggie said. "I'd better get started knitting a baby blanket."

They finished eating and passed around desserts. Rico paid close attention to Samantha, making sure she had enough of her favorite things, refilling her water glass whenever it got low, fetching her a napkin.

The Chihuahua continued to stare at him. *What's taking you so long? Have your way with her. You know you want her.*

Rico answered silently, getting really annoyed with RB. *I'm taking things slow. She's special. I'm not gonna fuck this one up.*

RB stared. *You're an animal just like me.*

You're a dog, I'm not.

Rico rubbed his forehead. He was going insane.

"So what do you think of our Rico?" Maggie asked Samantha. "Is he treating you nice? Returning the favor? We had a little talk about that over Scrabble one night." She turned to Rico. "Remember the L word?"

Rico cringed. She didn't mean "love," she meant "lick." Last February when they'd all been trapped in a snowstorm with no power, Maggie had suggested Rico remember to return the favor for this crazy-ass woman who was the host of a TV show that Daisy and Trav appeared on. He hadn't slept with the woman because she was into spanking, and he was hardwired never to hurt a woman, even if she asked him to.

"Rico has been…interesting," Samantha said.

"Oh, yeah?" Trav asked. "Interesting how? Is he playing Santa for you at home?"

"That was one time," Rico muttered.

He glanced at Samantha, who was blushing. Probably remembering when she'd sat on his lap and confessed her dreams. Right from the start, she'd been different from any woman he'd been with.

"You don't have to answer that," Rico said.

"He brought me roses and orange Tic Tacs and a love fern," Samantha said.

Rico's cheeks burned.

Trav pounced. "A love fern!" He smiled widely at Rico. "You don't say. Are we in *love*, Rico?"

He couldn't answer. He wasn't prepared to tell Samantha in front of a crowd. The Chihuahua taunted him in the corner.

Man up. Tell her you love her.

You're a dog. What do you know? You'll hump anything.

So will you.

I have standards.

"That's enough," Daisy said, breaking the staring spell between Rico and the dog. "You're embarrassing the poor man. And Samantha's our guest. So, Samantha, what do you do for work?"

The conversation turned to Samantha's work as a graphic designer, and Rico found he was learning more about this amazing woman. She designed book covers for children's books as well as doing some logo work on the side. She pulled a business card from her purse, and they passed it around. It had a cool block-letter logo with a fantastic image of hot air balloons in a blue sky with a kitten hanging by a string from one of the balloons. She was talented and beautiful. He listened carefully as Daisy drew more out of Samantha about her job, her travels—Spain had been a favorite—and her hobbies, she loved painting and photography. He stored it all away, each new fact a treasure.

Finally, the evening broke up as Daisy and Trav headed home to put Bryce to bed. Liz and Ryan left with them.

"Ready?" he asked Samantha.

She nodded. They said their good-byes and stepped out into the crisp, cold air.

"I hope you had a good time," Rico said, entwining his fingers with hers as they walked to his truck.

"They're wonderful," Samantha said. "What a cute dog too."

"He's an ass."

Her head snapped up. "What?"

"Nothing."

He opened the truck door for her and waited for her to get in, shutting it gently behind her.

"You think Rachel's pregnant?" she asked when he got into the driver's seat.

"Yeah. She's just like my sisters when they were pregnant."

"Why didn't she tell Shane?"

He shrugged and started the truck. "I guess she will now."

"I would never keep it a secret. I would shout it to the world."

That vision of Samantha round with his child bloomed in his mind again, and warmth spread through him despite the cold. "You want to be a mom?"

"Well, yeah. Not that I'm asking you to marry me and have kids. I mean, we just went out—"

"You could, you know. Ask me, I mean."

He glanced over. She was giving him a look somewhere between confused and shocked.

He put the truck in gear and pulled out into the street, kicking himself for jumping the gun. All those damn romance novels had him rushing to the happy ending. There wouldn't be a happy ending if she thought he was nuts.

"Never mind," he said. "I don't know why I said that. Too much eggnog."

"You drank water."

"Too much sugar, then."

Samantha went silent, and he turned on the radio. Harry Connick Jr. crooned "When My Heart Finds Christmas," and Rico finally knew what that meant. When they arrived at her parents' house, he parked and walked her to the front door.

"So I'll see you tomorrow for Christmas shopping. Ten okay?"

She bit her lip and nodded. He didn't touch her. He had to slow things down after that getting married remark. But then she leaned forward and kissed him softly on the lips. It was the first time a woman had kissed him first.

She pulled away, and he smiled goofily, glad he hadn't scared her away.

"I'll see you tomorrow," the future mother of his children said.

He grinned. "Tomorrow."

Chapter Ten

Samantha got ready for her shopping date the next morning cheerfully humming "Deck the Halls" as she remembered how attentive Rico had been, not slick at all. Sure, he'd been a little quiet but who wouldn't be with the O'Hares all talking over each other?

She slipped on a red V-neck sweater with her favorite perfectly worn jeans. She added a Christmas light necklace she'd picked up last year just for kicks and turned it on. Tiny multicolored lights glowed. She couldn't wait to see Rico again. Gone were his fake seduction routine and the phony tricks. The doorbell rang. Right on time.

"I'll get it!" she called.

She grabbed her coat and purse and opened the door. There he stood, handsome as ever. Some snowflakes drifted down, a dusting that made everything look fresh and new. She brushed some snow from his hair. "Hi."

"Hi." He smiled, and her pulse picked up. "Ready?"

"Ready." She stepped outside. "Where we headed?"

"I thought we'd brave the mall. Then we can stop at Something's Brewing Café for the best hot chocolate with homemade marshmallows you've ever tasted. It's Shane and Rachel's place."

"Sounds wonderful!"

They hit the mall and moved along with the crowd. Everything was so festive from the center court North Pole where Santa listened to Christmas wishes, to the giant two-story tree, to green garland hanging from the rafters with giant red ornaments. Every store was decorated with bright red bows and greenery. Christmas music played in the background. Samantha didn't normally like crowds, but with Rico at her side, she found she didn't mind at all. She'd already bought her sister and father a gift before this trip, but she still needed to find something for her mother. Rico took her to a cute boutique where he often bought presents for his mother and sisters. He bought his mother a scarf, and she did the same. He had good taste.

He stopped at the front glass counter where handmade jewelry was laid out on display. "What do you like?" he asked.

Her hand went to her throat. "You don't have to buy me a Christmas present. We just met three weeks ago."

"I want to." He gestured to the display.

"But I didn't get you anything," she protested.

He gazed into her eyes. "Being with you is my gift."

"Oh!" She swallowed hard, her throat tight with emotion. "That's just so…"

She couldn't find the words. She felt like she was living out her very own romance just like she'd always dreamed of.

"I know." One corner of his mouth kicked up. "Now pick something, or I'll just buy you this beautiful cricket pin."

She looked in the case. The cricket pin looked like a real cricket, the body covered in rhinestones. *Ewww.* "Okay, okay." She laughed. "I like those earrings." She pointed to a pair of earrings that looked like red water drops wrapped in a swirl of silver.

"You got it."

He bought the earrings and handed them to her. She put them on right away and admired them in the small mirror on the display case. "What do you think?"

"Beautiful," he said, only he wasn't looking at the earrings. He was looking at her in the mirror. She turned, and he gave her a quick kiss. "Come on."

He took her hand in his warm, calloused one, and they continued shopping. She noticed he took care in picking out the perfect gifts for his sisters, Elena and Maria. His love for his family shined through, and Samantha found she'd misjudged him. He was every bit as fabulous as her mother had told her. She learned about his family and how this year he'd be spending Christmas in Connecticut with his second family, the O'Hares. Selfishly, she was glad. She wanted to see more of him. She wanted time to pick out a gift for him too.

Bags in hand, they left the mall, and Rico drove to Clover Park for hot chocolate at Something's Brewing Café. They stepped inside the warm and cozy café painted a deep red. Large framed book covers decorated the walls. There was also a cozy reading area, lots of tables, and a cute kid corner in the back.

"Hey, Rico, Samantha," Shane called. He was working behind the counter with a couple of other employees.

"Hi!" Samantha called.

"Hey," Rico said. "Grab a seat," he told her. "I'll get the drinks."

She snagged a table for two in the back. The place was packed.

A short while later, Rico set a thick white mug filled with hot chocolate in front of her. A large square marshmallow floated on the cocoa topped with a whipped cream swirl and a sprinkle of cinnamon.

"It's almost too pretty to drink," she said.

"Drink up. It's good."

She sipped. Omigod. The whipped cream was light and sweet, the chocolate so rich and creamy. She'd never tasted anything so good.

"This is fantastic!" she exclaimed.

He grinned. "I told you. Shane just told me he's gonna be a dad. I knew it."

"Aw. That's great. I'm happy for them." She scooped out the marshmallow and took a bite. Heavenly! She'd never had a homemade marshmallow before. It was gooey and tasted like peppermint and the chocolate it had been soaking in. She pointed to her mouth and, after she finished chewing, muttered, "Omigod. So good. When are they getting married?"

He smiled. "The wedding's in two weeks, New Year's Eve."

"My mother would kill me if I was pregnant before the wedding," she confided.

"Good to know."

She flushed and took another sip of hot chocolate, feeling cozy and warm, like they were in their own little cocoon despite all the people around them. They talked comfortably about their favorite music and movies while they finished their drinks. Rico helped her put her coat on. She was so glad Rico had finally shown his true colors to her.

"Come back to my place?" he asked.

She nodded, her pulse racing. She wanted this, wanted him.

He flashed a smile, gave her a quick kiss, and led the way.

A short drive later, they arrived at his apartment. Rico stopped at the front door. "Wait here."

He went inside. Samantha waited. That was strange. What was he up to?

He came out a minute later, swept her up in his arms, and carried her over the threshold.

"Oh!" she gasped, surprised by the sudden pickup as well as the apartment. The place was dark, except for white twinkling Christmas lights strung all along the ceiling, along the archway separating the kitchen from the small dining area, and around a large ficus tree. Harry Connick Jr. crooned in the background. "It's beautiful!"

He gazed into her eyes. "You're beautiful."

And amazingly, she believed him. It wasn't a line. He actually meant it. About her. He carried her to the sofa and set her down. Sitting next to her, he stroked her hair, pushing it over her ear. He cradled her cheek and slowly leaned in. Samantha's eyes closed, and his lips met hers, kissing her tenderly. It was a long, slow, deep kiss, and warmth spread all the way down to her toes. His hand remained on her cheek, the other resting on her thigh, not moving, and she waited for more, wanted more. Until she finally couldn't take it anymore and pulled him down with her on the sofa.

He sat up and removed her necklace, which had been poking between them, and returned to kiss the side of her neck, feathering light kisses down to her collarbone, tasting her. He returned to her mouth, his tongue dipping in, and something in her snapped. She thrust her tongue in his mouth, her hands running all over him, suddenly crazy to have him. She tugged at his shirt, wanting it off, wanting nothing between them, desperate for skin on skin.

His mouth worked along her jawline, seeming in no hurry despite her frantic hands. He kissed his way up to her ear, where he murmured, "Samantha," as his clever hands undid the front clasp of her bra. He pulled back and slipped off her sweater and bra. Then he was kissing her again, his hands cupping her breasts as his rough fingers brushed back and forth across her nipples. She moaned, her hands fisting on the back of his shirt. Then his mouth dipped to suckle her breast, and the throbbing between her legs intensified.

"Rico," she said on a sigh.

He pulled back and gazed down at her breasts. "So, so beautiful." He kissed one breast, then the other reverently.

She pulled at his shirt again. "Take this off."

He stood, but instead of taking off his shirt, he pulled her with him and led her into the bedroom. She had a brief glimpse of a king-size bed with a black comforter before he was kissing her again and guiding her down to the bed. She pulled at his shirt again.

"This is all about you, baby," he murmured before kissing his way down her body. She quivered as he undid the button on her jeans and unzipped them. She lifted her hips, and he slid them down. She was instantly rewarded with a hot kiss over her center, his tongue pressing there through her damp panties.

She reached for him. "I want—"

"I know what you want," he said in the voice of the extremely confident as he slid off her panties. He nudged her legs apart and settled between them. He pushed in closer, his shoulders opening her as her legs were forced over his shoulders. She glanced down, she was spread wide open with his hot gaze on her most private area. Omigod was she really going to let him—

His fingers spread her folds, and he stroked her with his tongue. All thoughts flew from her brain. His mouth was magic, and she gave in to it as he used his lips and tongue, bringing her to the brink again and again, only to change to soft, light kisses that had her frantic and restless. She lifted her hips, silently begging for release, and then his fingers were inside of her, spreading her as his mouth sucked hard. She cried out as she convulsed with wave after wave of pleasure.

Finally she stilled. She felt him lean back, releasing her legs, and she lay there sated and boneless. Then he was kissing her softly, stroking her hair again. She opened her eyes. He was propped up on one elbow, looking down at her, still fully dressed.

She smiled. "That was amazing."

He grinned. "I could tell."

"Take off your clothes," she said. "We're not done yet."

He cradled her cheek. "That was just for you."

"But—"

His fingers touched her lips, shushing her. "*Mi querida*," he murmured.

The term of endearment shot straight to her heart. *My love*. In that moment she would've done anything for him. She reached for him and pulled, wanting his weight on her, wanting him inside her.

He didn't move. Instead he took her hands and held them. "I want to be a giver."

She sat up. "Me too."

He sat up and gave her a quick kiss. "This is something new for me. Just let me do this. Okay?"

Her brows furrowed in confusion. Did he not want her?

She put her bra and sweater back on, still tingling all over. He stood and handed her her panties that had fallen to the floor. She glanced at the front of his jeans where his erection bulged. He did want her. Why was he holding back?

She worked up the panties and jeans and leaned back to button them. Something jabbed into the back of her head. There, wedged between the pillow and the headboard was a book, *Highlander's Mission*. She held it up, puzzled. Had another woman left her book here? She owned this one. There was a really hot scene where the laird pleasures the heroine after her bath and then leaves her like that, wanting him.

Omigod. She went hot and cold all over. Rico was still pulling fake moves. Only now it was from books instead of movies.

She *so* wanted to be wrong about this. Her voice came out unsteady. "Whose book is this?"

His cheeks flushed. "It's my sister's!"

"I thought your sisters lived in other states."

"It's her Christmas present."

Then his words came back to her. When she'd thought he'd sounded so formal, *I'm a strong man, and I need a strong woman at my side*, it was the laird. Omigod, Rico was playing the laird. She felt the blood drain from her cheeks. Felt downright cold. She could barely look at him. She'd been played. Big time.

"You read this, didn't you?" she accused.

He looked guilty as all hell. "I peeked."

She stared at him, willing him to be honest with her for once. "Rico?"

He crossed his arms. "Fine. I read it, okay?"

"Why?"

His mouth formed a flat line.

"Why?" she hollered.

"Elena told me to, so I'd know how to make you feel special," he said quietly. His chin jutted out. "And it worked too! You loved it."

She stood on shaky legs. "Who are you? Who's the real Rico? Are you always putting on an act?"

"No! I just wanted to be what you wanted."

"I want someone who's real." She shoved a hand through her hair as anger rushed through her. "How can I trust you when everything you do is a carefully constructed show?"

He planted his hands on his hips. "What are you so mad about? You liked everything I did." He ticked off his good deeds on his fingers like it was a damn checklist on how to fool Samantha. "I talked about feelings. I took you shopping. I took things slow. I went down on you."

"That was from a book?" she exclaimed, her voice hitting a high note of indignation. She couldn't help it. She'd just had the most amazing orgasm of her life from Laird Blackwood.

He shrugged. "I usually receive. Those novels really spell out how to make it good for the woman."

"Omigod!"

He pinned her with a hot look. "Tell me that wasn't the best orgasm of your life."

"That's not—it's not," she stuttered.

He gave her a cocky smile. "It was, wasn't it?"

"Shut up!"

She headed for the living room and grabbed her coat and purse. She couldn't believe she'd let herself be fooled by him again. She was more mad at herself than him at this point. She should've known better. All the signs were there.

He appeared at her side. "Damn, Samantha, you are the most difficult woman I've ever met."

She gave him a hard look. "And you are the most deceitful man I've ever met."

They drove back to her place in dead silence. The cheerful carols on the radio grated on her nerves, mocking what she'd thought was a beautiful beginning with the most romantic, loving man she'd ever met. *I will not cry, I will not cry.* She made it all the way to her room before she broke down in tears.

Chapter Eleven

Rico headed for Garner's the next night feeling lower than low. He still didn't know why things had blown up in his face yesterday. He'd done everything right. Every damn thing women wanted, he'd done for Samantha. And still she got mad. There was just no pleasing her. Just when he thought he'd finally figured out this love thing, the rug was pulled out from under him. One thing was for sure, he wasn't taking any more advice from his sisters. What did they know? They were married with kids.

He opened the door of the restaurant, ignoring all the cheerful decorations and the happy hum of voices inside, and headed straight to the bar. Trav was there, waiting for him. He'd called his friend, unwilling to sit at home where memories of a naked Samantha haunted him.

"Hey," Trav said, pushing a Corona toward him.

"Thanks," Rico said.

"No problem." Trav took in his no-doubt sour expression. "So what went wrong? Tell Trav, he knows all, sees all."

Rico snorted and took a long pull on his beer. "I thought I did everything right."

"Yeah." Trav sipped his beer. "You know what? Forget her." Trav nodded like he was one of the fucking wise men. "There's plenty more where she came from."

Rico socked him on the arm hard. "Shut up!"

Trav laughed and clapped him on the back. "You finally got hit with the love stick. Hurts like hell, doesn't it?"

"Fucking love stick."

"I knew it'd get you sooner or later."

Rico's shoulders slumped. "What am I gonna do?"

Trav took a pull on his beer. "I'll tell you what you're *not* gonna do. Let her come to you. *Worst* advice ever."

Rico shook his head. That was the advice he'd given Trav when Daisy didn't immediately fall into his arms. Luckily Trav ignored him and was now happily married.

Rico eyed him. "So what's the best advice?"

Trav grabbed a handful of pretzels from a bowl on the bar. "Tell me the problem, and I'll tell you how to fix it."

If only it were that easy. There was no easy solution. He'd been up most of the night, replaying their time together, looking at it from all the angles. He really had done everything right.

He shoved a hand in his hair. "I don't know what the problem is! That's what's so frustrating. I'm telling you, I did everything right."

Trav shook his head. "When a guy thinks he did everything right, chances are he didn't. Tell me what she said, her exact words."

His leg jiggled up and down. "Which part?"

Trav popped a pretzel in his mouth and chewed. "The bad part."

Rico stilled his leg. "I told her she was the most difficult woman I'd ever met, and she said I was the most deceitful man she'd ever met."

Trav stopped, beer bottle halfway to his mouth. "That's harsh."

"I know! I'm not deceitful. I never lied to her."

Trav shot him a look. "No, Einstein, I meant you saying

she was the most difficult woman you'd ever met. Not exactly a love sonnet there."

Rico frowned. "Well, what about what she said?"

"That's harsh too. Damn, you guys are mean." He ate another pretzel. "I don't envy you."

Rico's spirits sank to an all-new low. "Me neither."

They drank beer in silence. Trav watched some hockey on TV while Rico stared at the bar, feeling hopeless. Dammit. Why did he have to fall in love with the most difficult woman on earth? It made no sense. He was an idiot. Stupid, stupid, stupid.

Trav's voice interrupted his thoughts. Rico had no idea what he'd just said.

"What?" Rico asked.

Trav raised a brow. "I said, if you didn't lie, why would she say you were deceitful?"

Rico played with the label on his beer bottle. There was no way he was going to admit to stealing moves from chick flicks and romance novels. "I dunno."

"Uh-huh."

Rico rolled his neck to relieve the tension there. "I *might* know."

Trav grinned. "Do tell."

"I'm not telling you that shit."

"Ooo-hoo-hoo, this just gets better and better." Trav chortled.

"Shut it."

Rico went back to his beer. He watched some game highlights, but all he could think about was Samantha. He'd lost her. There was no way she'd give him another chance. Nearly every date had ended in disaster. There was no hope. Zero. He blew out a breath of frustration and dropped his head in his hands.

Trav took pity on him. "Come on, it can't be that bad. Just

apologize for whatever you did, tell her you won't do it again, and ask her for another chance."

He was supposed to apologize for trying to make her dreams come true, promise not to do it again, and ask for another chance? Why in the world would she give him a second chance for that? She should want him to make her dreams come true. That's what didn't make any sense.

Women were so damn confusing.

~ ~ ~

Two days later, Rico mailed all the romance novels to Elena with a note: These were no help at all. He couldn't stand looking at them for one more minute. They taunted him with their hot sex and happy endings. He got in his truck and headed for home. Samantha wanted him to be himself? He was a guy who liked to drink beer and watch the Knicks. Was that what she wanted? A guy date, take it or leave it?

Wait a minute. She said she wanted him to be himself. He found himself turning around, heading toward Eastman, heading toward Samantha. What did he have to lose?

Rico didn't bother with flowers or rehearsing the right lines or any of that stuff he'd thought he needed to impress Samantha. She wanted him to be the real Rico, then that's what she'd get. He parked and walked quickly to the front door before he could lose his nerve. He knocked and waited, hoping it would be Samantha who answered the door.

"Hello, Rico," Mrs. Dixon said with a big smile on her face. "I had a feeling you would show up here. Samantha is very cranky. I'm sure you can help cheer her up."

"I'll try," he said.

"Sam, Rico is here for you!" her mother called up the stairs.

"Tell him to go away!" Samantha hollered.

Rico frowned. Mrs. Dixon huffed and marched over to the foot of the stairs. "You get down here right now and listen to what he has to say."

"He's a big phony, Ma!" Samantha hollered. "Tell him I said that."

"I can hear you!" Rico hollered up the stairs.

Mr. Dixon appeared in the foyer and came over to shake Rico's hand. "How ya doing?"

Rico shifted uncomfortably as he stood with the parents of the woman he loved, who was doing a very good job of making him feel lower than a damned cockroach. "I could be better. Can you get Samantha to come downstairs?"

Mr. Dixon held up a finger and walked upstairs.

Mrs. Dixon smiled at him. "So how is your mother?"

"She's well, thank you." He could hear arguing upstairs. "How are you?"

She rocked back and forth on her heels. "Good, good. Don't worry. She'll come down. She's just very stubborn."

"No kidding," Rico muttered.

Finally Samantha walked downstairs with her father right behind her, and Rico's heart thumped like crazy. She wore jogging pants and a baggy sweatshirt and her hair up in a messy ponytail.

She'd never looked more beautiful.

~ ~ ~

"Okay, I'm listening," Samantha said, arms crossed against him. She wouldn't be taken in by this phony one more time. She couldn't believe she'd kept going out with him even after all their fights and disastrous dates. After moping around the last few days, she'd vowed to be smart about romance and not just drift off to la-la dreamland, thinking she could have the kind of love you only found in fiction.

Her parents stepped back but didn't leave the room.

"Should we go somewhere more private?" Rico asked.

"Whatever you have to say to me you can say in front of them." She looked over to her parents. "I want them to hear what I'm dealing with."

Her parents looked at Rico eagerly.

Rico cleared his throat, looking pained. "Okay, here goes. I tried to impress you with all that romance stuff because I thought that's what you wanted, but you were right, that isn't me."

Samantha hmphed. "I knew it!"

"But this is me," Rico said. "I really want you in my life. You're all I can think about. Whether we're getting along or fighting, you're always right here." He tapped his head. "I thought I was having a heart attack because whenever I got near you my heart flip-flopped or squeezed or skipped a beat." He rubbed his chest. "Even now it's like a racehorse. It's love. The doc told me."

Samantha's brows shot up. She uncrossed her arms. Was there something wrong with his heart, or was he saying what she thought he was saying? She studied his expression. He looked totally and completely sincere. She felt herself weakening.

"You went to the doctor?" she asked. That must have been an awkward conversation.

"Shhh!" her mother scolded. "Go on, Rico."

He took a deep breath. "I love your smile, your talent, your goodness..." He paused, and Samantha found she could barely breathe because this felt real—this love he was trying so hard to express. He spread his arms wide. "This is the real me talking to the real you. So take it or leave it, the real me just wants to hang out at a bar with you, drink beer, eat wings, and watch the Knicks."

"I love the Knicks," Samantha said softly.

His eyes lit up, full of hope. "Really?"

She nodded as hope surged through her too.

He smiled. "I've never done that on a date before. I'm not trying to impress you. I'm letting you see the real me, and I hope you'll like who that is."

Samantha and her mother sighed at the same time.

"Don't leave the guy hanging," her father said.

Samantha laughed. "I'd love to watch the Knicks with you."

"I knew it! Mothers know." Her mother shook her finger. "I told you! Mothers know."

Samantha rolled her eyes; then she crossed to Rico and took his hand, not even caring she was wearing her old ratty comfortable clothes. If he could be himself, so could she. "Let's go."

Chapter Twelve

Samantha got into Rico's truck, smiling to herself. Finally she was getting the real Rico. And she liked what she'd seen so far.

He got in and turned the ignition. "For a minute there I thought I was going on a date with your whole family."

She laughed. "I'm sorry I made you say all that in front of them."

He pulled out into the street. "You're forgiven only because you're here with me now. Besides, I'm sure you'll run the gauntlet with my mother. My dad's no problem. He likes everyone."

She suddenly got worried. "Do you think she'll like me?"

He squeezed her hand. "Yeah, she'll like you. She'll want to check your permanent record for red flags but..." He looked over and grinned. "Any history of streaking? Please say yes."

She laughed. "No. I never went skinny dipping either."

"We can fix that. I've got a tub."

"Tell me it's not a hot tub. That would be just so—"

"Play-uh," he sang. "No, it's not a hot tub. It's a—" he lowered his voice comically "—*love tub* for special people named Samantha Dixon."

"You're too much."

"You'll let me know," he said in a husky voice that gave

her a thrill.

She crossed her legs, and he laughed. "Payback is a bitch," she told him.

He put a warm hand on her leg. "I can hardly wait."

When they arrived at Garner's Sports Bar & Grill, Samantha was starting to feel like she was on a first date without all the nerves. The restaurant was warm and welcoming, decorated with greenery and tiny multicolored Christmas lights strung along the ceiling. Rico seemed to relax the moment they left her parents' house. He was warm and funny, and if he'd been like this from the beginning, she would've fallen head over heels.

As it was, he had her at doctor. She couldn't believe he went to the doctor for a diagnosis of love. She'd fallen for him too. No man had ever tried so damn hard in so many crazy ways just to be with her.

The wings arrived, and they each took one, hot and spicy and crispy, just like she liked them.

Rico wiped his mouth with a napkin. "So how do you like Garner's?"

"I love it. Good wings too."

They watched the Knicks, ate hot wings, drank cold beer, and Samantha had never had a better date.

Rico turned to her after they finished the wings. "You're a mess." His thumb wiped at her chin, then her lower lip. "Hell, I'll just kiss it off." He leaned over and kissed her, drawing her lower lip into his mouth, sucking it. Heat pooled through her body. She kissed him back, her hands gripping his shirt, and the kiss got hot and heavy fast.

He pulled back. "You want to get out of here?"

She jumped off the bar stool. "Yes."

They walked out of the bar holding hands. The night air was cold and crisp. Main Street was lit with white lights that arched over the street. More white lights wrapped along the trees that lined both sides of the street.

"It's so beautiful here at night," she said.

Rico stopped and gave her a quick kiss. "You're so beautiful. And that's not a line."

"Oh, Rico!" She threw her arms around him.

He wrapped his arms around her waist and swung her around.

She laughed. He set her down but didn't release her. He just stood there, his arms around her waist, smiling down at her.

"I shouldn't have complained so much about your romance stuff," she said. "You meant well."

"No, you were right. I was borrowing lines and faking my way through. But now it's from the heart."

She swooned. Then they were kissing again, right on Main Street, under the twinkling white lights.

He pulled back with a groan. "My place?"

She beamed at him. "Yes."

They walked hand in hand to his truck. He did the whole open door, shut it gently behind her thing, and she was glad to see that his manners were here to stay. It was so gallant.

His place was a short drive away. Once he unlocked the door to his apartment, she threw herself at him, and he staggered back.

"You don't waste any time," he said with a grin.

She tried to climb him like a fire pole. "We've wasted enough time."

"Samantha?"

She kissed her way up his neck. "Hmm?"

His warm, rough hands ran up and down her bare back under her sweatshirt. "I want you so bad but…" He trailed off as she sucked on his earlobe.

"You got me," she said before kissing him again.

He groaned into her mouth and hauled her against him.

But he wasn't moving to the bedroom or getting naked, and that was a problem.

She pulled away and met his eyes. "What's wrong?"

He flashed a quick grin. "Nothing, believe me. I'm ready." They both glanced down at the massive erection bulging through his jeans. "But I wrote you a song, and I really wanted you to hear it before we…make love."

Make love. Omigod, could he be more sweet? She ran to the sofa and sat down. "I can't wait to hear it."

He headed over to his guitar, and she sighed happily. The guitar playing was real, and now she was going to get her very first serenade dedicated to her.

He settled on the sofa next to her and strummed a few notes, tuning it. He was so sexy when he bent over his guitar like that. She waited for his melodic voice to sing to her in Spanish.

Beh-beh-beh. He glanced at her as he started to play. *Beh-beh-beh.* The beat was fast and loud. She sat up straighter. Rock 'n' roll. Then he belted out the lyrics:

"Love hit me like heart failure
I thought I was gonna die
Samantha! Samantha!"

She slapped a hand over her mouth, torn between crying and laughing. This wasn't like any of his other songs. Her eyes welled up. That was exactly what made it so special.

He went on:

"Things were tough
Then they were rough
Samantha! Samantha!
What would I do without a girl like you
Can't wait to find out what's in store

Samantha! Samantha!"

Her heart filled with love as he belted out her name, pouring his heart and soul into the song. He finished and turned to her. She bit her lip to keep from crying.

"Did you like it?" he asked.

She nodded and felt a tear slip away. "I loved it."

"What's wrong? You're crying." He set the guitar down and pulled her into his arms.

She smiled through her tears. "I'm just happy."

He wiped a tear off her cheek with his thumb, kissed her tenderly, then folded her in a tight embrace. Her whole body relaxed in his warm, strong arms.

He pulled back to look at her, stroking her cheek. "Okay?"

She nodded. "What else did you learn from those romance novels?"

He barked out a laugh. "What are you into? Werewolf style, old-school Scottish, billionaire dominance, low-down country, reformed bad boy—"

She lifted a finger. "I'll take that last one."

He grinned. "You're looking at him."

"You are *not* bad."

"You said I was a player."

"You were!"

"Not anymore." He kissed her gently. "Just you, Samantha, only you."

"Oh, Rico," she breathed. "Enough talking. Get naked. Now!"

"That's my line," he said on a laugh. He lifted her off his lap and stood. "Just remember you wanted bad boy," he reminded her as he peeled off her sweatshirt.

She threw her arms around him. "I do, I really do."

And then his hands were everywhere as his mouth pressed hard on hers, demanding entry, and she opened for him. His tongue thrust inside, and she lost herself in his taste, in the rough stubble scraping her as his warm lips devoured her. Her bra sprang open, then it was off, and before she had time to pull his shirt off, her pants hit the floor. His hand thrust between her legs, pressing against her dampness, and she gasped. He ripped the panties off in one quick pull, and her eyes flew open.

She was completely naked, and he was still fully dressed.

"Get those damn clothes off now," she growled.

"You want this?" he asked, peeling off his shirt.

Her mouth went dry as she took in the full effect of a half-naked Rico. He *was* like that unicorn. She didn't know such beautiful muscular men existed in real life. She ran a hand over one warm pec and down his rippling abs. He pulled a condom from his pocket and dropped his pants and briefs. She forgave his obvious plans for their night in light of his obvious, thick, hard desire. She gulped.

"And this?" he asked. She goggled over his colossal erection as it stretched the condom.

"Yes," she breathed.

Then he grabbed her, turned, and pinned her back against the wall. And there was nothing but him, his musky scent, his skin burning into hers, his mouth pressing into her. He slid his hands under her bottom, lifted her, and then with one hard thrust he was inside, stretching her, making her ache. She panted.

"Wrap your legs around me, baby," he crooned into her ear.

She did. But then he surprised her by carrying her like that off to the bedroom. "I thought I was getting the wall banging," she said, trying to hide the disappointment in her voice.

Rico groaned and tightened his hold on her. "The wall's too hard for you. I want silk against your skin."

Then they were in the bedroom, and he shoved the cover aside. He released her to lay her down gently on silk sheets. She ran her hands along the sheets. She'd never known a guy who had silk on his bed. "You have silk sheets?"

He rose up over her, settling between her legs. "I like softness too."

He kissed her tenderly, then moved along her cheek, nuzzling into her neck.

"This doesn't feel like bad boy," she pouted.

He stilled.

Maybe she shouldn't have said that. But she'd gotten so excited that she was finally going to get the bad-boy experience. Even better, the bad boy with a tender heart, the perfect combination.

He lifted his head to gaze into her eyes, a smile playing over his lips. Then he cradled her face with one hand. "This is what a bad boy feels like when he's fallen in love."

Her heart squeezed. She felt that love soul deep. She smiled up at him. "I think I'm falling for you too."

"You think?"

"I might need a bad boy to sway me."

He dipped his head and nipped her bottom lip, and her hopes soared—bad boy was back. He pulled back long enough to yank her down, away from the headboard, then grabbed her leg, lifting it and setting it over his shoulder.

"Bad boys like a woman who goes along for the ride," he told her with a hot look that had her throbbing in anticipation. He lifted her other leg and set it over his shoulder.

"You talk too much," she said, goading him on.

"I talk too—woman!" He grabbed her hips and drove into her, hard and fast, so she could barely catch her breath. The position forced her wide open, and she threw her head back in surrender as hot waves of pleasure drenched her, making her clutch at his back, her nails scraping, wild for him as the thrusts rubbed against some pleasure spot on the inside that made her crazy. Her moans seemed to drive him on as he pumped harder and faster.

"Touch yourself," he growled.

She did without hesitation, too far gone for any inhibitions with this man. He watched her, his eyes dilated with desire, as she pleasured herself while he thrust deep and hard inside her. She panted, eyes wide open on her very own sex god, already on the brink.

"Come for me," he commanded.

At the words, she came violently, the room going out of focus as pleasure crashed over her. And then he was pounding into her for what felt like a never-ending pleasure ride as her insides coiled and tightened again. With a guttural groan, he reached his own climax, and she took in every last shuddering thrust until her body clamped down as she broke in a rush, crying out his name.

They stayed like that for a moment while she shuddered from aftershocks as he throbbed within her. He released her legs and crashed down onto the bed next to her.

He took her hand. "Was I too rough?"

She grinned. "I liked it. Next time I want werewolf style."

He groaned. She looked over. His eyes were closed, and he was smiling. "You're gonna kill me. You're really gonna kill me."

"The doc said it was just love," she teased.

He opened his eyes and drilled her with them. "You think that's funny?"

She bit back a smile. "Maybe a little."

He grabbed her and hauled her on top of him. She let out a squeal of surprise. He kissed her tenderly. "You won't be laughing when I'm done with you."

She smiled cheekily. "I certainly hope not."

He stroked her hair behind her ear. "I love you so damn hard."

"I love you too. Kiss me, my romantic hero."

He did, and it was with real, true love.

Epilogue

Rico brought Samantha to the O'Hare Christmas Eve party, feeling like he'd won the fucking lottery. Samantha was perfect for him. First off, she was a Knicks fan, she liked beer as well as wine, and she liked to shake it up in the bedroom. He smiled to himself thinking of their recent billionaire-into-light-bondage adventure. She was beautiful, smart, artistic, loving, the perfect future mother of his children.

To think they never would've found each other if not for their crazy mothers and that matchmaking Maggie. He felt like getting down on his knees and kissing their feet in gratitude.

Maybe not that far. But he did hope to give his mother the wedding and grandkids she'd prayed for. He squeezed Samantha's hand and gave her a quick kiss before he rang the bell. After this, they'd be heading to her parents' house.

Trav opened the door, wearing the Santa hat with mistletoe hanging off the pom-pom. "Ah, you're under the mistletoe," he told Samantha as he leaned toward her.

Rico's hand slammed into Trav's chest. "Don't even think about it."

Trav laughed and made kissy noises at Rico. Samantha giggled.

They stepped inside, and the Chihuahua ran by, mistletoe

headband in his mouth. Probably going to destroy that offender of his dignity. Rico breathed in the scent of pine and hot chocolate and cinnamon. Maggie came up to them in her Santa hat with two more in hand. Actually everyone was wearing Santa hats. Christmas Eve tradition.

She plopped one on his head and one on Samantha's. "Merry Christmas, you little lovebirds!" she exclaimed. "I can tell you did the deed, you're glowing."

Samantha turned bright red. Rico laughed.

This time instead of the chipmunks, Julio Iglesias crooned Christmas carols—Jorge must have picked the music—as everyone sat around the cozy living room with a cheerful fire. There was eggnog, mulled cider, and hot chocolate with peppermint sticks sticking out of it. All his favorite people were here, his second family—Maggie and Jorge, Trav and Daisy, Ryan and Liz, Shane and Rachel. Trav's son, Bryce, sat on the floor, banging the hell out of a toy drum.

"Our little drummer boy," Daisy said with a smile.

Rachel handed Rico a wrapped gift. "Don't open it until you get home," she said with a wink. "It's that one we talked about."

It was in the shape of a book. He felt himself flush. It was one thing for Samantha to know he read romance novels, but he sure as hell didn't want that getting around to anyone else.

"Thanks," he managed. He left to quickly slip it into the inside pocket of his jacket, out of sight.

When he returned, the party was moving to the dining room for appetizers. He always did eat well when Shane was around. The food was gourmet—baked artichoke dip, Caesar salad on garlic toast, shrimp with spicy dip, sugar and cinnamon spiced nuts, fried risotto balls with toasted pistachios, cheese tarts. Shane explained what each dish was before they started to help themselves. Rachel stayed in the far corner of the room, sucking on a peppermint stick.

After everyone settled at the table with their food, Shane joined Rachel across the room.

"We have an announcement," Shane said.

"I'm pregnant!" Rachel exclaimed.

Everyone clapped and congratulated the happy couple even though not one of them was surprised.

"When are you due, honey?" Maggie asked.

"August seventh," Rachel said.

"Liz," Ryan prompted.

"Now's not a good time," Liz said, smoothing her hair back over her ears. "Congratulations, guys, I'm so happy for you."

"Thanks," Rachel and Shane said in unison. Shane leaned over and kissed her.

"Liz," Ryan said sternly.

"No," Liz said out of the side of her mouth. She smiled sunnily. "Everyone go back to eating."

No one ate. Everyone stared at Liz. She rolled her eyes and shot Ryan a dark look. He grinned.

"Tell us," Maggie said. "The suspense is killing me. You don't want a death on your hands on Christmas Eve!"

Liz shook her head. "Okay, okay! After much thought and soul searching, Ryan and I have decided to start a family."

Everyone clapped and congratulated the happy couple.

"Liz," Ryan warned. "I'm gonna say it if you won't."

Her hands fluttered in the air. "Okay, fine! I'm pregnant too!"

Maggie whooped. "Thank you, Santa!"

Everyone laughed. Ryan wrapped an arm around Liz and kissed her cheek.

"Wait, when are you due?" Rachel asked.

"I planned it around the school year so I wouldn't have to leave my class," Liz said. She was a third grade teacher at Clover Park Elementary. "I'm due June twenty-second."

"Tell them what you didn't plan, sweetheart," Ryan said.

"Twins!" Liz exclaimed. She shook her head. "I am in for it."

"Mazel tov!" Rachel exclaimed. Liz jumped up, and they hugged each other.

Rico's throat felt tight. He took Samantha's hand and squeezed. Everyone was downright merry as they talked and laughed and ate, full of promise for the future. It moved Rico. He wanted that for him and Samantha too. Soon.

After they finished eating, everyone went back to the living room, chatting and laughing. Rico pulled over a couple of chairs and sat by the glowing Christmas tree with Samantha, wanting her to himself.

"I have to warn you," he said. "My mother's flying up to meet you over New Year's."

Samantha smiled, and his heart squeezed. "Perfect. My mother can give her my dowry."

His eyes widened. "You have a dowry?"

"Apparently."

"Then we should definitely marry." And right then, right there, filled with love for her, and surrounded by the friends that he loved, Rico went down on one knee. Because when it was right, it was right. Even if they had just met weeks ago. It was *destino*.

"Rico, what are you doing?" Samantha exclaimed. But then

her eyes welled up, and he knew she was his.

Conversation stopped. The only sound was the soft Christmas music and Bryce playing his drum.

"Hush, Bryce," Maggie said. "Here, play with this."

The room went quiet. All eyes were on him.

He took her hand in his. "Samantha, I love you with all my heart. Will you do me the honor of becoming my wife?"

She jumped up. "Yes!"

Everyone cheered. Tears stung his eyes, but they were the happy kind. He stood and kissed her smiling lips; then he wrapped her tight in his arms. This was the kind of love that lasted. This was their very own happy-ever-after. And he couldn't have picked a better woman if he'd tried.

Which he hadn't. *Thanks, Ma!*

Coming in 2015!

The Clover Park STUDS series centers around three geeks—Barry, Dave, and Will—who unleash into studs with the love of the right woman. It's like *The Big Bang Theory*, but hawt.

Stud Unleashed: The Prequel

Computer nerd and frozen yogurt store owner, Barry Furnukle, hasn't had a girlfriend in fifteen months, two weeks, and three days. Not that he's counting. And even though his new beautiful neighbor, Amber Lewis, is way out of his league and has a beefy, tattooed boyfriend, he can't help but wish she'd notice him. After Barry sees Amber's boyfriend with another woman, he slips coupons to his fro-yo shop under her door, thus beginning a friendship that Barry hopes will bloom into so much more. He just has to figure out a way to prove he's more than the geek next door.

Barry smiled and took a sip of his coffee as he sat for the first time at Amber's kitchen table. Her cell vibrated on the counter. She jumped up to check it.

She frowned and returned to her seat.

"Bad news?" he asked.

"Rick cancelled on me. He's already tired from work and just wants to head home after. He's a bouncer at a bar in Norhaven."

Bouncer, that he could believe. And also a big liar. He'd just seen him sucking face with another woman at Garner's, which wasn't work or in Norhaven. Jerk.

"You and Rick been going out a while?" he asked casually.

"Four months." She drank her coffee, still looking upset.

"He cancel on you a lot?"

"I understand. It would've been late by the time he got here. It's fine."

He should let it drop. He really didn't want to hear more about Rick, and he didn't want to let slip what he knew, but he couldn't seem to help himself.

"You and Rick exclusive?" he asked. "Pretty serious?"

She narrowed her eyes. "Are you hitting on me?"

"No, no, no." He shook his head to emphasize it. "Absolutely not. My curiosity got the better of me. Forget I said anything." He took a sip of coffee. "This is good."

She stood abruptly. Damn. He'd overstepped.

"I didn't mean anything by it," he said.

She got out two shot glasses. "You want a drink, Barry? Cuz I could sure use one."

"Uh, sure."

He watched as she slammed around in the cabinets emerging with a cocktail shaker, a couple of liqueurs, and vodka. Now this was getting interesting. She expertly mixed the drink like one who had a lot of practice.

"Did you used to be a bartender?" he asked, impressed with her quick movements.

She shook it all up. "Smart guy. Yeah, I bartended in college once I was legal." She lined up two shot glasses and poured. It smelled a little like coffee. He checked the labels. Amaretto and coffee liqueur. Sounded tasty.

She handed him a glass and held hers up. He clinked it against hers. She downed the shot, and he quickly followed suit. Yum. He shook his head. Bit of a kick there at the end.

"What was that?" he asked.

"Screaming orgasm."

He sputtered. "Been a while since I had one of those."

She winked. "Been a while since I had the drink kind."

An image flashed through his brain of Amber in full

ecstasy, screaming as she came. Sweat broke out on his forehead. He discreetly adjusted himself under the table. She poured them another shot, and they clinked glasses again.

"Down the hatch," he said. They drank at the same time. Warmth spread through him. He rolled his neck, feeling looser already.

She slammed her glass down. "Why do men suck? Just be honest with me."

He was used to women sounding off to him, the nonthreatening friendly guy, so he put it out there, the cold, hard truth. "Because they don't appreciate what a wonderful woman you are."

She blushed. "Stop. You hardly know me." She traced the table with a fingertip. "How am I wonderful?" she asked softly.

"Well, just look around. This place is warm and full of vibrant colors." *Like you.* "That tells me you're a passionate woman who loves life."

He worried for a moment that he shouldn't have said "passionate," even though he knew instinctively she was exactly that, but then she met his eyes and grinned. "I like you."

"Thank you, I like you too." He smiled goofily, a little buzzed. "Plus you're an artist. A very talented one at that. Not many people can do what you do. If I tried to do what you do, it would look like a chimpanzee got into the paints."

She smiled.

He lifted a finger. "And you're smart. You caught on right away to the brilliance of my birding app."

She laughed, and he grinned.

"You're kind," he said, serious now. "Look how you welcomed in your new neighbor. Like you knew I needed a friend."

He really did. It wasn't easy to move into a tight-knit small town, the outsider. Sure, people were friendly, but he didn't hang out with anyone on a regular basis. And it had been fifteen months, three weeks, and one day since he'd had a girlfriend. He really had to stop counting. The numbers racking up were doing a number on his ego.

She took his hand and stared into his eyes. He felt like they were connecting on a deep, deep level. It felt so good to hold hands. He could do this all night.

"You are my friend, Barry…" She paused. "What's your last name?"

"Furnukle."

She wrinkled her cute little button nose. "Really?"

"Why would I make that up?" One side of his mouth quirked up. "My real first name is Barrett if you like that better."

"Barrett," she repeated. "Barrett Furnukle." She made a face. "Okay, if I call you Bare?"

He flexed his fingers like claws and growled. "Like bear?"

"Sure, okay. Bare, you *are* my friend. From this day forward—" she lifted her shot glass dramatically "—oh. It's empty." She poured them both another shot. "Raise your glass, Bare." She waited until he did. Then she touched her glass to his. "From this day forward, you are my friend. Deal?"

He smiled, a smile that didn't feel altogether genuine because he already knew he wanted her as much more than a friend. Yes, she was way out of his league, but he had needs, dammit.

"Deal," he said.

They drank on it. She smiled brilliantly. "I am toast. Come watch TV with me."

He stood, a little wobbly. Three shots was a lot for him. He usually only had a couple of beers once a week. And he'd had a beer earlier.

She waved her hand and veered unsteadily to the side. "Ooh, wait. Let me get some cheese. I love cheese." She grabbed a bowl of cheddar cheese cubes from the fridge and headed for the sofa. He followed.

"You like zombies?" she asked.

He didn't. He liked sci-fi movies, especially old movies with laughable special effects. Zombies gave him nightmares. What was so appealing about dead people walking around with various body parts rotting off them?

"I love zombies," he said.

"Great! I've got seasons one through three of *Zombie Bonanza* on DVD." She hit play on the DVD remote.

They ate cheese cubes and watched zombies while Barry contemplated doing one of those casual stretch-and-arm-around-her-shoulders moves. An hour later, Barry still hadn't made a move and had more grotesque zombie images burned into his brain than he knew what to do with. Still, he wasn't complaining because, without any prompting from him, Amber had just curled up against his side, which allowed him to easily and quite naturally slip an arm around her shoulders.

She smiled up at him, her eyes soft. "You're like a best girl friend," she mumbled before conking out.

Best *girl* friend? She must still be tipsy. He certainly hoped so. He was a red-blooded *man* with a lot to offer. Sure, he didn't have Tattoo Guy's machismo, but he had smarts, he had money, he had…a raging hard-on. He had needs, *dammit.*

He also had moves from his mother's romance novels he was dying to try out.

That's right. In his boredom kicking around her house this past year, he'd picked up a few books his mom had left lying around. No shame in that. *Carnal Werewolf* had been especially interesting.

He let out a breath, enjoying the feel of her cuddled up against him. He'd figure out how to move things to the next level tomorrow.

The Clover Park Series

The Clover Park STUDS Series (Coming in 2015)

Acknowledgments

Big hugs to my family, who cheer me on and pepper me with lots of future book ideas. My brain and heart are so full! Thank you to Tessa, Pauline, Mimi, Shannon, Kim, Maura, and Jenn for all you do. Virtual chocolate to all my readers! I hope you have as much fun reading these stories as I do writing them!

About the Author

Kylie Gilmore was lucky enough to discover romance novels at a young age as they were strewn all over the house (thanks, Mom!). She writes quirky, tender romance with a solid dose of humor. Her Clover Park series features the O'Hare brothers, three guys you'd definitely have a drink with and maybe a little more. Look for her new spinoff series, The Clover Park STUDS Series, in early 2015.

Kylie lives in New York with her family, two cats, and a nutso dog. When she's not writing, wrangling kids, or dutifully taking notes at writing conferences, you can find her flexing her muscles all the way to the high cabinet for her secret chocolate stash.

Thanks!

Thanks for reading *Kissing Santa*. I hope you enjoyed it. Would you like to know about new releases? You can sign up for my new release email list at Eepurl.com/KLQSX. I promise not to clog your inbox! Only new release info and some fun giveaways. You can also sign up by scanning this QR code:

I love to hear from readers! You can find me at:
kyliegilmore.com
Facebook.com/KylieGilmoreToo
Twitter @KylieGilmoreToo

If you liked Rico and Samantha's story, please leave a review on your favorite retailer's website or Goodreads. If you write a review, please send me an email at kylie@kyliegilmore.com so I can thank you with a personal email.

36020055R00075

Made in the USA
Lexington, KY
04 October 2014